Dear Reader,

Home, family, community and love. These are the values we cherish most in our lives—the ideals that ground us, comfort us, move us. They certainly provide the perfect inspiration around which to build a romance collection that will touch the heart.

And so we are thrilled to have the opportunity to introduce you to the Harlequin Heartwarming collection. Each of these special stories is a wholesome, heartfelt romance imbued with the traditional values so important to you. They are books you can share proudly with friends and family. And the authors featured in this collection are some of the most talented storytellers writing today, including favorites such as Brenda Novak, Janice Kay Johnson, Jillian Hart and Patricia Davids. We've selected these stories especially for you based on their overriding qualities of emotion and tenderness, and they center around your favorite themes—children, weddings, second chances, the reunion of families, the quest to find a true home and, of course, sweet romance.

So curl up in your favorite chair, relax and prepare for a heartwarming reading experience!

Sincerely,

The Editors

ROXANNE RUSTAND

lives in the country with her husband and a menagerie of pets, many of whom find their way into her books. She works part-time as a registered dietitian at a psychiatric facility, but otherwise you'll find her writing at home in her jammies, surrounded by three dogs begging for treats, or out in the barn with the horses. Her favorite time of all is when her kids are home—though all three are now busy with college and jobs.

RT Book Reviews nominated her for a Career Achievement Award in 2005, and she won the magazine's award for Best Superromance of 2006.

Roxanne loves to hear from readers! Her mailing address is P.O. Box 2550, Cedar Rapids, Iowa 52406-2550. You can also contact her at www.roxannerustand.com, www.shoutlife.com/roxannerustand or at her blog, where readers and writers talk about their pets, www.roxannerustand.blogspot.com.

HARLEQUIN HEARTWARMING

Roxanne Rustand

A Home in Hill Country

Harlequin®

TORONTO NEW YORK LONDON
AMSTERDAM PARIS SYDNEY HAMBURG
STOCKHOLM ATHENS TOKYO MILAN MADRID
PRAGUE WARSAW BUDAPEST AUCKLAND

Recycling programs
for this product may
not exist in your area.

ISBN-13: 978-0-373-36447-3

A HOME IN HILL COUNTRY

Copyright © 2011 by Roxanne Rustand

Originally published as BACK IN TEXAS
Copyright © 2005 by Roxanne Rustand

This edition published by arrangement with Harlequin Books S.A.

For questions and comments about the quality of this book
please contact us at Customer_eCare@Harlequin.ca

® and TM are trademarks of the publisher. Trademarks indicated with
® are registered in the United States Patent and Trademark Office, the
Canadian Trade Marks Office and in other countries.

www.Harlequin.com

Printed in U.S.A.

A Home in Hill Country

To my dear mom, whose love and encouragement
always meant the world to me.

CHAPTER ONE

THE ONLY WAY Ryan Gallagher had figured he'd ever come back to Four Aces Ranch was if he arrived in a government-issue casket.

Returning home on his own power had never been part of his plans.

Now, standing at the entryway of the main house, he glanced over his shoulder at the deeply rolling land stretching to the horizon. Every gnarled cedar, every rocky outcropping stirred a flood of memories he couldn't hold at bay.

He'd been gone fifteen years, barring two brief trips home to see his brother married and his grandfather buried. It hadn't been long enough.

Ryan shook off his reservations. *Just a few months, maybe less.* How could this be any harder than Ward 57 back at Walter Reed?

Turning back to the ornately carved oak door with Four Aces Ranch written in sweeping script between images of champion quarter horses and prize cattle, Ryan knocked before letting himself in.

Nothing but the best, his father had always

said. From the livestock and land acquisitions, to every ostentatious detail of his massive brick house, Clint Gallagher still wasn't finished trying to impress the world.

His decades as a Texas State Senator had never been enough for him.

"I don't believe it." Adelfa stood transfixed in the middle of the foyer on her way to answer his knock. The elderly housekeeper's dark eyes filled with tears as she drank in the sight of him from head to toe. "*Madre de dios!* I never thought I'd find you at this door!"

Steeling himself against the pain radiating through his shoulder, Ryan enveloped the stocky Latina in a hug. "And nothing could be better than finding you're still here."

He released her, surprised by his reluctance to step away from Adelfa's familiar scent—cinnamon and the Chanel he always sent her for Christmas and birthdays. "You still make this place home," he added, brushing a kiss on her wrinkled brow. "Only you."

"Your father could not always be here when you boys were young." She frowned, as quick to defend her employer of forty-some years as she'd always been to stand up to him. "He is a busy man…an *importante senador*."

And to her, that made everything right. She was, Ryan realized with chagrin, every bit as loyal as his fellow Rangers, even if her loyalty was misplaced. "So, is Clint here?"

"Si." Adelfa cast a glance over her shoulder, her brow furrowed. "But…he is not such a happy man tonight."

Ryan threw his head back and laughed for the first time in months. "Tell me when that *wasn't* true."

She clucked at him, her mouth a stern line. "He has many responsibilities. Phone calls. Visitors. The newspapers—aye, they still send their reporters out here, looking for a good story."

"Clint always knew how to use the press," Ryan retorted dryly. "The reporters were either in his pocket or wanted to be."

Adelfa rocked back on her heels and crossed her arms over her ample chest, muttering rapid-fire Spanish phrases under her breath.

He caught every word and grinned at her. "I agree. He won't listen to anything I say, and this visit will be a big mistake if I just upset him."

A deep blush worked its way into her plump cheeks. "Some things, they just don't got a fix to 'em," she murmured.

"For Garrett and Trevor's sake, I'm staying for a couple months. By then, we'll either have this ranch straightened out, or Dad and I will have dueled out in the desert."

Her *harrumph* spoke louder than words. "So you have talked to your brothers?"

"Not yet, I understand they ran out of options, and figured I was their best bet. They asked Leland to track me down." The certified letter from the Four Ace's lawyer had caught up with Ryan in Georgia several weeks ago. "Maybe they think I'm less likely to walk out than someone hired off the street."

"You and your father are both stubborn and strong as two bulls." There was a note of pride in Adelfa's voice as she sized him up. "For nothing more than that, you would stay now to prove him wrong."

"I don't much care what he thinks about me, and I'm not intimidated by what he says. You know how well we get along." Ryan gave her a quick wink. "For that reason alone I'm probably the best person for the job. I hear the ranch is in financial trouble."

At the faint jingle of spurs, Ryan turned and found his middle brother, Trevor, grinning at him from the doorway, dressed in his usual faded Levi's with a plaid Western shirt stretched across his burly chest. He held a dusty Stetson.

Ryan extended his hand, but Trevor ignored it and gave him a bear hug before stepping back for a thorough appraisal.

"Long time," he drawled. "You looked a mite

peaked the last time I saw you. Musta been that fancy gown…or maybe it was because those nurses moved a lot faster'n you could."

"I barely remember those first days at Reed." Ryan closed his eyes against the flashes of fuzzy images…the beep of his morphine drip…the glare of fluorescent lights, day and night. Somewhere, in that fractured catalog of memories, he had a vague picture of Trevor's worried face as he bent over the bed. "You *were* there, right?"

Trevor snorted. "Not for long. You ordered us to go home and leave you in peace. You were so surly about it, day after day, that the nurses finally encouraged us to keep in touch by phone."

Ryan winced. "Must've been the medication."

Trevor shot him a wicked smile. "Bein' unwanted and all, we finally had to turn tail and go home in disgrace."

"I don't know what to say, except that I'm sorry."

Adelfa searched Ryan's face. "They took good care of you, I hope. Good food? A good bed? We worried about you, every day."

"Well…not a whole heck of a lot," Trevor added. "Me and Garrett figured you were just too mean to die."

Adelfa gripped Ryan's forearm for a minute, as if for reassurance, then lumbered back to the kitchen, muttering in Spanish.

"She lit candles for you at her church," Trevor said in a low voice. "She had a little shrine here, on the sideboard in the dining room, and had candles going there, too, and she never said grace at a meal without adding prayers for your healing." His voice broke. "It's good to see you again, pal."

Ryan swallowed the unfamiliar lump in his throat. "Same here."

"And Dad—" Trevor looked away. "Well, he was in the middle of trying to get some bill passed. He couldn't make it out to Washington, D.C. with us, but I know he was concerned, and he did make some phone calls."

Concerned? Ryan laughed. "I hope that didn't interfere with his schedule."

Trevor glanced over Ryan's shoulder into the house, his eyes troubled, then he hitched a thumb toward the main horse barn. "Maybe we should go have a talk, before he finds out you're here. Got a minute?"

Ryan shoved his battered duffel bag to one side of the doorway with his boot. "My time is yours."

Trevor led the way to the pine-paneled office in the main horse barn, just inside the double doors.

"Looks like you're doing well." Ryan nodded toward shelves crowded with quarter horse championship trophies and framed Superior and Register of Merit award certificates. "Last time I was here, the trophies only filled *one* wall."

"I spend a lot of my time on the road now. We hit most of the major show circuits west of the Mississippi." Trevor shrugged. "It's good for business."

Ryan sauntered over to the five-tier racks of show saddles and the glittering rows of silver-encrusted show halters, bridles and breast collars hanging from padded hooks. "Well, I'll be." He rested a hand on the custom-made saddle that had been his, a lifetime ago. "I'm surprised this is still here."

"Of course it is. It's yours." Trevor motioned to a couple of leather barrel chairs in front of the cluttered desk, then tossed his hat on one of them, propped a hip on the edge of the desk and rubbed his face. The premature gray in his dark hair and the deep lines creasing his cheeks made him look far older than thirty-two.

"It's good to have you back. Things have been tough here—real tough. What did Leland tell you in the letter?"

"Mostly things I already heard. That Oscar moved away and left the financial records in a mess, then the new foreman embezzled a lot of money." Ryan leaned back in his chair. "Did anyone check out Oscar to see if he was involved?"

"He went back to Mexico and we lost track of him, but we all thought he was an honest man.

Experienced hand with cattle, though he managed just basic record keeping and never did understand that dinosaur of a computer. Hardly capable of pulling off a complete embezzlement scheme."

"And the next man?"

"Dad fired Oscar's replacement four months later." Trevor shook his head in disgust. "Lucky, or Nate would've had more time to steal us blind. Leland says we'll never know the full extent of that loss."

"Nate *Cantrell?*" Ryan stared at him. "I knew there were problems, but never heard all the details."

"You haven't been back since it happened. I thought I wrote you...but, with you halfway around the world most of the time, maybe that letter never caught up." Trevor's brow furrowed. "Crazy isn't it? A local guy, doing something like that to people he knows."

"All I remember is that he and dad had occasional business dealings over the years." The name brought other, less welcome memories, but none Trevor needed to hear.

"After Nate, Dad hired a string of business managers who either quit or were fired, and now he's trying to do it himself. He's trying to get *me* to do it," Trevor amended. "I never went to college. I don't know anything about accounting—and I'm out working with the cattle from dawn to dusk as it is. I've tried, but he gets impatient. Then he works on it himself and…" He took a deep breath. "You know about him, right?"

"That he's an arrogant old coot? That he's probably making your life miserable?"

Trevor stood and wandered over to the saddle racks, where he absentmindedly began polishing the silver cantle plate on a Billy Royal cutting saddle with the cuff of his shirt. "His eyes, Ryan. He won't admit it to anyone. I only know because I happened to see a billing slip from his last ophthalmology appointment. He's got macular degeneration. He's also got high cholesterol and a bad heart, but I sure haven't had any luck making him go in for his checkups. He's long overdue—and one of these days, he's gonna drop in his tracks."

"All this at *sixty?*"

"His vision upsets him the most. He'll spend hours in his office in the house poring over bills and reports, but I can tell he's struggling. It's no wonder he didn't catch what was going on—he can barely see to read."

Ryan sat back in his chair trying to absorb the enormity of that news. Clint was well-known as a powerful force in state and local politics; a wheeler-dealer who was ruthless in his business dealings and who carefully cultivated a broad spectrum of cronies to help him meet his ends.

What was it like for him, now that he faced the potential loss of his independence?

"Can't the lawyer help out with all of this?"

"Leland is on retainer. Dad consults him on financial matters sometimes—investments and so on—and he has limited power of attorney to oversee major business decisions if Dad isn't available. He doesn't cover day-to-day management. It might be different if he was always in town, but he lives in San Antonio and just comes to his satellite office in Homestead a couple days a week. I can't do it all, no matter what Dad thinks. Frankly, I don't even know where to begin. So—" Trevor ended on a long sigh "—we've had overdue notices. The hunting lease program is a mess. Records are missing. Dad is land rich and cash poor right now, and last winter he missed a chance to pick up a big piece of property that borders the Four Aces."

"He needs *more* land?"

"You know Dad." Trevor shook his head. "Money. Power. Land. He wants it all, but the K-Bar-C was far more than that. It controls the aquifer that supplies a large percentage of our land. It was tangled in foreclosure for over a year. When it finally came up for sale, he couldn't pull enough money together in time. That still rankles him to no end."

"I'll bet." Ryan gave a short laugh. In Texas,

prime access to a substantial underground aquifer could mean the difference between bankruptcy and success. "He's never been one to lose happily. What about Nate—has he been caught?"

"He died a few months after being fired. Leland worked for a couple weeks on the bookkeeping disaster Nate left, then gave up and hired a forensic accountant and a private investigator. They discovered that money disappeared through cash withdrawals, and large checks to fictitious companies in Austin and Dallas. Some was filtered into an account in Llano, in the name of a nonexistent crop-spraying service. That doesn't account for all of it, though…not even close, from what we can tell."

"Was any of it recovered?"

Trevor snorted. "Very little."

"Do you have a copy of that report?"

Trevor hitched a thumb toward a bank of drawers behind the desk. "In there—but it really doesn't say any more than we already knew."

"What about the sheriff? Didn't he investigate?"

"Dad said he wanted to keep this quiet until he had enough evidence." Trevor lifted a brow. "Personally, I think he was more worried about the election year ahead—didn't want voters thinking he'd mismanaged his own business. And knowing Dad, he probably has a few financial affairs he doesn't want brought to light."

"But when Nate died, surely—"

"Nope. The P.I. discovered that Nate had quite a gambling problem, so it must have disappeared on the gaming tables. There was no paper trail indicating he'd transferred the money to anyone else." At a sharp rap on the doorjamb, Ryan looked over his shoulder.

Clint stood there, as tall and imposing as ever, his lean, hard face reddened and his eyes flashing with anger. "Guess I'm part of this here discussion, wouldn't you say?"

No *hello,* no *good to see you.* Which was, Ryan reflected, no surprise at all. "Hey," he said lazily, lifting a hand from the arm of his chair in greeting.

"Adelfa said you two were out here." Clint glared at his sons. "You should have come to my office."

Trevor cleared his throat. "I just—"

"I haven't seen my brothers in a good long while, Dad." Ryan swung out of his chair and met Clint's steely expression head-on, knowing that any show of sympathy or support for the old man would likely spark a tirade. "When I run into Garrett, I plan to have a good, long visit with him, too."

An uncomfortable silence lengthened until at

last Clint stalked into the room and scraped a chair against the floor before dropping into it. He gave Trevor a narrowed glance. "I understand you and Garrett sent for Ryan. It wasn't necessary."

"Sounds like it was," Ryan said mildly, leaning a shoulder against the wall. "I understand y'all need some short-term help to get everything back in order. After that, you can bring in a new business manager, and I'll be out of here."

"Interference, that's what it is," Clint snapped. "You had no right."

"Trevor didn't hire anyone behind your back, Dad. He and Garrett asked me to come home for a while and pitch in." Ryan gentled his voice to a lethal, dead-calm tone. "I know I have no stake in this place anymore, and I sure know how you feel. Believe me, I wouldn't have come back if I hadn't felt I owed it to my brothers to make sure their legacy was secure."

OVER THE YEARS he'd captured infiltrators. Rescued team members from impossible situations. Tracked, caught and interrogated enemies who would have welcomed death and the chance to take him right along with them.

Convincing his arrogant and irritable father to get into his own Lincoln the next morning and driving him to town—winning a ten-dollar bet with Trevor in the process—had been one of the greatest challenges of all.

Glancing at the sign over the door of the small clinic, Ryan stepped out onto the street and pocketed the car keys. "I'm sure this Dr. Hernandez is competent, Dad. We were lucky to get you in this morning."

Clint climbed stiffly out of the car and straightened to his full six-foot-one height, his hand still on the open door of the car. From his thick white hair to the tips of his custom-made Lucchese boots, he exuded an imperious air of power— the Texas kind, an unshakable belief that he controlled everything in his part of the world.

The tense silence in the car on the way to town had proved that nothing in the rocky relationship between them had changed over the passing years…and it never would.

"Doc Grady died five years ago, and there hasn't been a doctor here since. What does that tell you?" Clint leveled a glare at Ryan. "This guy probably couldn't get a job in a real town—or got chased out of the one he was at. If he's any good, why would he come to a town like this?"

Excellent point. Ryan looked down the deserted sidewalk, taking in the boarded-up storefronts and empty parking spaces. The only signs of life were a couple of old gents dozing on benches in front of the massive, limestone courthouse across the street, and a handful of dusty pickups nosed up to the local diner.

The Homestead, Texas, city limits sign still claimed a population of 2,504, but he'd bet a good thousand of those people had long since fled the area, for better jobs and a brighter future.

"You're not having heart surgery here—just a quick checkup and some lab work," Ryan said dryly. He opened the door of the clinic, and jingled the car keys in his pocket. "I'm sure the guy can handle that much. Get this over with, and we can go home. Unless you want to drive clear into Austin, fight traffic and sit in a busy waiting room all day for the same thing."

Clint stalked to the clinic and brushed past Ryan as he went inside, muttering under his breath. He thrust an impatient hand toward the empty receptionist's desk. "See? No one's here."

"But the door was open and the lights are on. Adelfa called and talked to someone here just an hour ago."

The decor was nearly the same as it had been back when Ryan used to come here. Curling brown linoleum. Faded Western prints on the walls. He eyed the same hard wooden chairs he'd sat on as a kid, knowing that after a few minutes in one of them, he'd have trouble walking.

An inexplicable, eerie sensation prickled at the back of Ryan's neck as he walked farther into the room. He spun back to look at the open front door. There was nothing there.

From behind him, he heard soft footsteps come down the hallway leading to the exam rooms. A rustle of papers.

"Hi, can I help you two?"

The quiet voice slid through him like a bayonet.

As if from miles away, he heard his father say, "You gotta be kiddin' me."

And then he felt the earth shift beneath his feet.

CHAPTER TWO

HER VOICE WAS FIRM, with no hint of the old, familiar flirtatiousness, but those six, simple words had the impact of a round from an M-16.

Ryan turned slowly, wishing he'd lost this morning's bet with Trevor, and looked into the eyes of the woman who'd left him fifteen years ago.

It took him a good five seconds—nearly a lifetime—to find his voice.

"I...thought you'd moved away from here, Kristin," he said, dropping his gaze to her white running shoes, snug jeans and white lab coat opened to reveal a Texas A&M T-shirt, before finally meeting her eyes again.

She acknowledged Clint with a nod, but her attention was on Ryan; her shock apparent when she saw the thin, ragged scar trailing from his temple to the corner of his jaw. "Years ago, I—I heard you were missing."

He hitched his good shoulder. "Yeah, well... maybe for a while."

"For a while, people even thought you were..."

"Dead? Not quite." At her stark expression, he regretted his flippant answer. Apparently even Kristin Cantrell had feelings, somewhere in her cold, dark heart.

"S-so you've moved to the ranch, then?" She paused. "Everything's okay now?"

"Fine. But I won't be here long." He stared into her light blue eyes, so startling in contrast against her long, dark blond hair and late-summer tan. His gaze unconsciously slid to her bare ring finger before he jerked it back to her eyes.

She was more beautiful than she'd been at nineteen. Maturity had brought sharper definition to her cheekbones and an elegance that had been just innocent girlishness before. He nearly laughed aloud at that. *Innocence.* As if.

Long ago—not that he cared—he'd heard she'd married Ted Peters, a banker's son they'd both known in college. Not a surprise, really. For her, it had always been about money.

Old memories, best left forgotten, he thought grimly. None of them mattered anymore.

She found her voice again before he could, though her face was pale and she seemed to have an overly strong grip on the documents she held. "A woman called to make this appointment for a physical, but with her accent I didn't catch the name clearly. I—I didn't realize—" she cleared her throat "—that it was for you."

"It's my father. He needs—"

"*Absolutely nothing* from another Cantrell." Clint leveled a frosty glare at Kristin, then stalked to the door. "I'll be in the car."

An awkward silence lengthened as they both stared after him. Finally, Kristin looked at Ryan, embarrassed, and moved to the reception desk where she ran a finger down a column in the appointment book. "Apparently neither of you knew I was going to be working here. Um…we have other openings, if you think he'd be willing to come back."

Ryan frowned, remembering her dreams of becoming a pediatrician. Her vow to never return to Homestead. "You…manage this place?"

"I'm a physician's assistant, now. We're formally opening this satellite clinic on Tuesday, but I've seen a few walk-ins early. Dr. Lou— Louisa Hernandez—will just be here on alternate Wednesdays."

Clint probably wouldn't want to see a female physician, either, but it might be worth a try… especially if Trevor or Garrett could be conned into the trip. "Next week, then?"

"He could see me anytime. We haven't even started scheduling appointments yet, so the book is open." She smiled regretfully. "If he prefers the doctor, he'll have to wait two weeks, or he'll need to drive clear over to the main clinic in San Antonio."

"While I'm home, I need to get him set up locally. It'll be that much easier for Trevor when…" Ryan hesitated. Clint would resent his sharing personal information if he didn't end up a patient here. "When Dad gets older. Just give him another appointment on Tuesday morning, and I'll make sure he gets here."

"I know this is difficult for all of us. Tell him that he doesn't need to worry, I won't ever refer to the past." The hint of sadness in her voice was almost believable. "Has he been under the care of another physician?"

Ryan nodded. "Apparently someone in Austin, but from what Trevor says, Dad has never been good about keeping appointments and taking his medications. He probably needs complete lab work in addition to a checkup."

Kristin wrote on an appointment card and held it out. "Nine o'clock."

Ryan flinched as he reached for it, the sharp pain in his shoulder reminding him about the empty prescription bottles in the glove box of his truck. Taking a deep breath, he fought the urge to close his eyes and lean against the wall until the dizziness passed.

"Are you all right?" Kristin stepped around

the desk and hesitated, her hand hovering above his arm.

He gave the slightest shake of his head, wishing he could back away and get out of there without another word, but well aware that he probably wouldn't make it to the door.

"Can I get you something? A glass of water?"

He didn't try to disguise his irritation, hating his weakness, his inadequacy. Hating the attention and sympathy it always drew. "Leave…me…alone."

She grabbed a chair, settling it behind him and gently took his other arm. "*Sit,* unless you want to leave here in an ambulance. If you go over on this hard floor, you'll end up with a concussion."

Pride and stubbornness kept him upright, his anger subsiding as the sensation of vertigo faded. "I'm fine. Really."

"Right. And I'm Mary Poppins." Kristin took a step back and folded her arms across her chest, clearly now in professional mode. "Tell me. What happened to you?"

He managed what he hoped was a semblance of a smile. "Just a little…altercation."

"A *little* one." Her voice was filled with disbelief. "How long ago?"

"Six months. It's nothing."

"Right. And I bet you sleep like a baby, no

problems at all. Are you in physical therapy? Do you take anything for pain?"

"I—" He swallowed a sharp reply, suddenly tired of being defensive. Tired of the whole deal that had jerked him out of active service and into a world of surgery and pain, and empty promises from docs who didn't have the guts to tell him the truth. "I do need some refills. Can a Texas P.A. write prescriptions?" he asked, more roughly than he'd intended.

"Yes, after you've established a relationship with that clinic."

"So I have to wait until I can see the doc?"

He stifled a sigh. He could get along without most of his medications just fine, but the pills helped him keep moving during a bad day. And now and then, the Percocet was his only relief when the burning, throbbing pain in his shoulder or knee kept him awake until three in the morning.

When he finally fell into troubled sleep on those nights, the nightmares would return, and then he'd lie there wishing that he'd died in that hellish place instead of Tony and Dave and all the others. He rarely gave in and took the meds. But when he truly needed them...

She must've read his thoughts, because she touched his arm and smiled. "I can take care of this, easily."

She handed him a clipboard from the counter. "Fill out this health history. If you don't have your medical records, you'll need to sign a release so we can request them."

He wished he'd just walked out the door. Confidentiality of medical records was mandated by federal law. But sharing personal information— having *anyone* read about the injuries that made him weak and useless now—still rankled.

And though there was nothing between them any longer, revealing those details of his life to Kristin Cantrell was a thousand times worse.

"I…have a folder of photocopies out in my truck."

"Good, then. I'll start a chart while you get it. After you fill out this form, I'll take your vitals and you'll be set." She lifted a brow. "Are you game?"

There was a distinct challenge in her voice and her businesslike manner. She'd been such a sweet, shy little thing in college, wide-eyed at the world around her. Now she wore a much tougher veneer, and he could almost imagine her taking over a platoon.

In a few minutes he was back inside. He handed her the paperwork, then followed her down the empty hallway to an exam room. "Are you the only person here?"

"Our clinic nurse starts Tuesday." She motioned him to the exam table, then flipped open the folder. "Wow. You were at Walter Reed?"

He nodded.

"So this was no little bar fight, then." She took a deep breath, clearly stunned. "You should go down to the Kerrville VA Medical Center. It would cost you a lot less, and—"

"No."

"But—"

"I saw the doctor at Reed just last week. I don't need to see anyone else." His feisty doc back at the hospital had been sure Ryan would refuse to seek ongoing medical care, so the man had provided just enough capsules for the trip west, along with printed orders on what had to be represcribed by a local doctor. "Look, my dad's outside talking to Arlen Enfield, but he won't want to wait long."

"Enfield…the former mayor?" She glanced up at Ryan, then started jotting something on the margins of the medical report. "Nice guy. I met him last winter, when I visited here."

Enfield was tall, sophisticated. Urbane, with a propensity for saying just the right thing, but *nice* wasn't the word Ryan would've used.

Who could forget the subtle animosity between the two men? Both wealthy ranchers, they'd been political rivals over the years. Intelligent, driven and competitive, they reminded him of two old dogs circling each other with hackles raised. "Can we make this quick?"

"Fine." She took his blood pressure, weight and listened to his lungs, asking questions and jotting notes in a chart as she went.

She was pure, cool professionalism. But with every touch of her delicate hands, he had to force himself to be still, to betray no reaction. He hoped she didn't sense his tension.

Only after he'd walked out the door of the clinic was he finally able to haul his thoughts back to the present.

Trevor would definitely need to bring Dad into the clinic on Tuesday, because seeing Kristin again was the last thing Ryan wanted.

No Ranger with a 60mm mortar could have done a better job of destroying his heart.

KRISTIN WAITED until she heard the door of the clinic close behind Ryan, then leaned her forehead against the cool, smooth wall of the waiting room. His new patient chart still in her arms, she willed away the tears burning behind her eyelids.

She'd expected challenges when she decided to move back to Homestead, with a new career. A new home. A nine-year-old son who considered Central Texas the last place on earth he wanted to live. And a town that held bad memories from her early childhood.

But she certainly hadn't expected to run into Ryan Gallagher on her second day here.

For years, she'd known he was a Ranger, involved in highly dangerous operations in the Middle East. Last year, when she'd been back in town for her dad's funeral, she'd overheard someone mention that he was still there, and that he rarely ever showed up in Texas.

There was nothing between them, not anymore. But discovering that he'd been airlifted out of Afghanistan as a "Critical 4"—on the verge of death—just months ago, had filled her with sadness.

Scanning the grim surgical reports in his medical folder had made her feel worse. His well-muscled, six-foot-two body had suffered multiple, serious injuries that time would never totally heal.

His lean, darkly handsome face was the same. The nearly black hair she'd once loved to touch. The piercing blue eyes and strong masculine jaw.

But the twinkle in his eyes had died, along with his quick wit and his born-and-bred Texas cowboy manners, leaving behind a stranger. A hardened and dangerous soldier, one who'd survived all those years.

With luck, Ryan hadn't seen the sorrow and sympathy in her eyes over all he'd sacrificed in the line of duty, or noticed how his arrival had thrown her off balance.

But no matter what he thought, no matter what she'd once prayed for, there was no going back. She had too much at stake during the next six months to even think about old loves or new beginnings. Cody's future depended on it.

CHAPTER THREE

"SO...WHAT DO YOU THINK of your new place?"
Miranda Wright, Homestead's mayor, climbed
out of her blue pickup and pulled an overflowing
welcome basket from across the seat, then closed
the door.

Her dog—some sort of golden Lab mix—hung
its head out the window and watched sorrowfully
as Miranda flipped her long ponytail over her
shoulder and handed the wicker basket to Kristin
with a flourish. "Dusty really wanted my mom's
Texas Pecan Kisses—there's a dozen of 'em in
here—and I swear that dog will do *anything* for
a cookie."

Kristin grinned at her over the huge red bow
tied at the top of the handle. "Thanks. Want to
come in and see what I've done so far?"

The tall brunette checked her wristwatch and
frowned. "Just a few minutes. I've got to get
home, load up and deliver hay to a sheep farmer
near Llano by five."

"The guy down at Tanner's grocery tells me you
raise the best peaches in the entire area." Kristin

shook her head in amazement as she pulled open the yard gate set in the low limestone wall encircling the house and ushered the other woman through. "You must be the busiest person in Loveless County."

Miranda laughed. "I don't handle it all alone. My mother, Nan, takes a very active part, and we usually have at least one family working for us." She stopped in front of the small two-story house and propped her hands on her hips. "I think this is one of my favorite old houses in this area. A little paint, replace some windows on the ground floor, and this place will be lovely, don't you think?"

"Yes, I do. I already have a lot of plans, for when I have the money and the time." Kristin led the way up onto the wraparound porch and into the front room. "We've just unboxed the living-room things and still need curtains, but it's starting to feel like home."

Just minutes ago she and her son, Cody, had shoved their old leather couch and love seat into position, with the couch facing the fieldstone fireplace and the love seat at a right angle to it, flanked by oak end tables. A lacy white afghan over the back of the love seat covered the worst of the scuffs, and a pile of pillows on the couch covered some deep scratches.

Miranda brushed a hand across one of the stained glass lamps on the end tables, admiring the deep jewel tones. "These are so pretty. Family heirlooms?"

Kristin felt herself blush. "A consignment store in Austin, I'm afraid. There weren't many things to pass down in my family."

"Lovely all the same." Miranda nodded in approval. "It's great finding treasures like these and being able to save money while you're at it."

She moved over to a wall and peered at the thermostat. "Have you checked the heating system? The water and appliances? We sent a handyman out here to look at everything before you arrived this week, but I always want to make sure."

"Perfect, far as I can tell." Kristin bit her lip. "I owe you all so much. I never thought I'd be able to afford a place of my own. Not like this one... and especially not in my hometown."

"Life comes full circle, doesn't it?" Miranda smiled kindly. "The town is delighted to welcome young families to the area. The homesteading program is a two-way street, really. We offer people a chance for new beginnings. In turn, we bring in new life for our community and our schools. With your medical skills you'll be a great asset here."

"Can I offer you tea? Coffee? A soda?"

Kristin moved toward the kitchen, but Miranda shook her head. "I have to be going, but don't forget those cookies." She winked. "Best on the planet."

"Thanks so much. I know we'll love them."

"If you catch her at a good moment, my mom might even share her secret recipe." Miranda chuckled. "Is there anything you need before I go—any questions?"

"Not right now, I guess. The contract is pretty straightforward." Kristin hesitated. "I love this isolated setting. The view is incredible, and the peace and quiet is wonderful. Neighbors would be fine, too, though. Will there be any more people coming out this way?"

"Eventually. We've got around twenty-five thousand acres to work with, but we don't want to rush. Finding the right people is more important to us than just giving it all away." She tapped a fingertip against her lips and thought for a moment. "You and your son are the third family to arrive, but we'll have more arriving nearly every month for a while. Most of the parcels in this area are between twenty and a hundred acres. You share a property line with a remote part of a privately owned ranch, though, so that will help you maintain your privacy."

Kristin grinned. "That's perfect. I promise, I'll meet every stipulation to the letter."

"I'm not sure if you knew, but this place was called Cedar Grove Farm. The man who lived here before raised goats, had a few horses and did a little truck farming—vegetables and peaches, mostly."

From the doorway leading to one of the main-floor bedrooms, Kristin caught a flash of movement. "Cody?"

He dutifully came back around the corner, all gangly nine-year-old shyness, the blush on his fair cheeks nearly matching his bright auburn hair. He held one hand behind his back.

Something to check on as soon as Miranda leaves. "This is Miranda Wright. She's the mayor, and she heads up the committee that brought us here. Can you tell her thanks?"

He ducked his head, avoiding eye contact with either of them, mumbled something that might have been a *thank-you,* then raced around the corner.

"I'm sorry, he's usually much—"

"No problem." Miranda waved away the apology as she started out the door. "I'm sure this move has worn him out, and most little guys are shy with strangers, anyway. We'll meet again soon."

Kristin leaned a shoulder against the door frame and watched Miranda stride to her truck and drive away, feeling suddenly melancholy.

"New beginnings," she said softly to herself. "Something I've needed for a long, long time."

Though those new beginnings weren't going to be entirely smooth. Cody had been acting out a lot more over the past few weeks. And her bank balance was close to zero.

On top of that, some people in town who'd started to welcome her, had stopped when she'd introduced herself. It was as if they'd recognized her, and their smiles had faded.

She'd been just a child when she and her mother had fled this town over twenty years ago, but her father had stayed...and obviously there were still people who remembered the Cantrell name.

And that, she realized with a heavy heart, could make living here more difficult than she'd imagined.

CODY GLARED at the TV in the corner of the living room, wishing he could throw the whole thing out the window.

There were a million places they could've moved to, but Mom had chosen this one—an old house surrounded by high, rocky hills in the middle of nowhere. A place where exactly one channel came in clearly, without a satellite dish, but only if a guy stood with a hand on the top of the TV and thumped it now and then.

What did kids do around here? No sidewalks. No playgrounds, unless you drove all the way into town, and that was a good ten miles. No neighbors with kids and dogs and tree houses.

The only *good* thing about moving was that he'd gotten out of Mrs. Morgan's class back in Austin. She'd been mean. Always blaming him for the whispering at the back of the class, or for the spitballs thrown at the kids in the front row. He'd had a time-out almost every day, and that *totally* stank.

At least his new teacher seemed nice. She smiled a lot, and came over to ask him if he needed help, because she said he'd have to catch up to everyone else. She smelled pretty good, too...not like Morgan, who must've taken a bath in perfume every morning and had breath worse than Ben's old dog next door.

Cody listened to the thumping and scraping coming from upstairs, where Mom was unpacking more boxes and pushing furniture around, then he went out onto the porch and leaned over to brace his elbows on the railing. Dropping his chin into his hands, he stared out at the hills that seemed to roll on forever, clear over to where the sun was starting to drop lower in the sky.

There were supposed to be big snakes out here. Big, *big* rattlesnakes, and coyotes and even armadillos—like the ones in his favorite Jan Brett storybook. Maybe there was even a mama armadillo parading through the low cedar bushes and sagebrush right now, followed by a train of little armadillos.

Dad called armadillos "speed bumps" because you always saw them flattened along the Texas highways, but the possibility of seeing a live one sent Cody off the porch in two big leaps.

With a last glance over his shoulder at the house, he hopped over the low stone wall and jogged past Mom's pickup, stopping to survey the possibilities. Where, exactly, did armadillos like to go?

To the right of the house he could see the tops of a big stand of trees growing past the next hill. They were probably those huge, shady old live oaks that Mom was always admiring, because she said they could be hundreds of years old.

Surely, with a hot sun overhead all day—even though it was almost the beginning of September—an armadillo would like a shady place to rest.

Grinning, he broke into a run.

NOT AGAIN. Kristin frantically raced through the house one more time, checking the closet and even beneath the beds.

Since the divorce, Cody had been unpredictable—clinging one minute, rebellious the next. He sometimes hid from her when he was upset, apparently finding some sort of satisfaction in crying quietly by himself and ignoring her pleas to come out.

But this time, she sensed the emptiness of the house. Where could he have gone? The western sky was deepening from lavender into purple and indigo. The sun had set. And already, the chilly night air was settling in.

"Cody!" she called out, searching around the yard for any sign of him. In exasperation, she widened her search to include the old, empty barn and the small, one-car garage too narrow for her modern vehicle.

The lane leading out to the highway was empty, the powdery caliche limestone revealing only tire tracks. But Cody could've skirted the lane and gone across country on some adventure without regard for the temperature, approach of nightfall or the fact that he had absolutely no knowledge of the area.

And just within the boundaries of her own twenty acres, he could so easily be lost. Running, now, she shouted his name as she searched farther and farther from the house.

Only a distant owl returned her calls.

Her heart pounding, she slowly turned in a full circle, watching for any sort of movement.

Nothing.

With a cry of frustration, she ran back to the house to grab her cell phone and call for help. *Did*

911 even work out here? Surely there'd be local police, or a county sheriff, and maybe even a dog that tracked.

She lunged up the steps and breathlessly pawed through the packing materials on the kitchen counter until her fingers curled around the familiar shape of her cell phone.

She flipped it open to punch in the numbers, then stared in disbelief at the faint message blinking on the screen.

Low battery.

Her hand at her throat, she slumped against the counter, her lungs raw from the exertion. Then she hunted through the clutter again until she found her truck keys.

At a sharp knock at the door she froze. She was a woman alone in an unfamiliar, isolated place... though that barely registered.

I don't have time for this! I've got to find my son.

She took a deep ragged breath, gripped her keys in one hand and hurried to the front window.

A big gray horse stood placidly in her yard, tied to the gate. A *horse?*

The front door opened with a crash, and Cody's excited voice echoed through the house like a gift direct from God.

"Mom! Mom! I got a ride on a horse! And it was

huge, and beautiful and the cowboy said I could ride again if you say it's okay. Mom!"

Overwhelmed with relief, she turned away from the window, still gripping the curtain for support.

Cody barreled into her just as she caught sight of a tall stranger inside her front door, silhouetted against the lamplight of the living room.

"I...I..." She closed her eyes and wrapped Cody in a tight hug until he wiggled free, then took a steadying breath and looked up to the door. "W-who are you?"

The man stepped into a pool of light, and she found herself staring into Ryan Gallagher's eyes.

"How easily you seem to forget," he said coolly. "At least you're consistent."

Cody anxiously tugged at her sleeve. "Please, Mom. He says I can have another ride. Please? You said we'd get horses when we moved, and this one is *beautiful*. Please, Mom!"

Kristin stared down at him, then shifted her attention back to Ryan. "I don't understand. Why are you here?"

"You city folks might let your kids run, but you can't do that here. Not with a child who doesn't know the area or how to get back home." His tone was excessively patient, as if he was trying to explain something to a person with limited mental capacity. "Your boy was over a half mile into the Four Aces."

"I've been searching for him *everywhere.* I just came inside to call for help."

Ryan glanced at the TV, which was on and inexplicably now coming in clear as a bell. He raised a brow as he turned back to her, clearly imagining that she'd simply been sitting in here watching reruns. "If I hadn't been riding this evening, Cody might've kept going in the wrong direction, in a remote pasture that holds several hundred unpredictable mother cows and calves. He could've been trampled, or developed hypothermia by later tonight."

Kristin shuddered. "He is never to leave this property. He knows that."

"We've also got hunting leases on that land. A careless hunter might see a sudden movement and shoot before thinking." Ryan glanced down at the boy and paused. "Keep him home, and make sure you know where he is."

His obvious assumption of negligence rankled for a split second, but he was right. She shouldn't have let Cody out of her sight, and she could only feel gratitude and heartfelt relief that Ryan had come to his rescue.

"I can't thank you enough for bringing Cody back," she said quietly. "If there's ever any way I can repay you—"

"Please, Mom," Cody begged. "Can I ride again?"

Kristin gently took his beloved face in her hands. "The answer is no. Absolutely no. You ran off, and you never said a word. You left the yard, which is against the rules, and this nice man had to interrupt his evening to bring you back."

She straightened and pointed to the stairs. "One hour, time-out. *Now.*"

His eyes filled with sudden tears, but he slowly trudged away, his head bowed, looking for all the world like someone headed for death row.

"I'm really sorry for all your trouble," Kristin said, turning back to Ryan. "I promise—"

But he was already gone.

CHAPTER FOUR

THE MOMENT KRISTIN opened the door of her aunt RaeJean's beauty salon, she knew it was a mistake to stop by on a busy Saturday morning… *especially* with Cody in tow.

"Oh, my!" RaeJean Barker exclaimed, tossing aside her comb and brush. "Aren't you just as cute as a sack full o' puppies today?"

Cody cringed against Kristin's side and tried to wiggle away, but RaeJean was faster.

She barreled up to him, gave his shoulders an affectionate squeeze, then tapped under his chin with one crimson-tipped fingernail. "And aren't them just the prettiest eyes? Just like your momma's." She winked at him as she pulled a shiny fifty-cent piece out of the pocket of her pink uniform jacket. Flipping it high in the air, she caught it and offered it on her outstretched palm. "You look like a cowboy in need of a Coke."

He stared up at her, his mouth open, and Kristin prayed he wouldn't comment on RaeJean's flame-red curls or turquoise eye shadow. She was, undoubtedly, the most colorful person he'd ever seen.

"Can you say thanks?" Kristin prodded.

He mumbled something and dropped his gaze to his Nike runners, his ears pink.

RaeJean beamed her approval as she hiked a thumb toward the back of the salon. "Minifridge is back there. Or you can go to the vending machine next door, right in front of the saddle shop. They got more flavors, but it's not near as cold."

Cody nodded shyly, then shuffled across the room as if he were crossing enemy territory.

No wonder.

Nothing much had changed here since Kristin's childhood. Fluffy pink curtains hung at the windows, pink flamingo wallpaper still covered the walls. Ornate, gold-framed mirrors topped the two cluttered workstations, matching the heavy gold wall sconces and frames on the pictures of outdated hairstyles.

The explosion of baroque decorations and bawdy femininity, coupled with the sharp scents of bleach and perm chemicals, nearly took Kristin's own breath away.

She glanced over the row of women settled under the six dryers at the back of the room, who were watching them with avid interest. Women who, when they walked out the door, would be wearing identical, tightly curled helmets reminiscent of the 1960s. Whatever the request, Rae-Jean always proceeded to do exactly what she thought best, and that was the one style she did for "women of a certain age."

Which explained, unfortunately, the number of do-it-yourself haircuts in town and the exodus of the well-to-do to the upscale shops in San Antonio.

"Um…maybe Cody and I should stop back later. I thought you'd be closing about now."

"Uh-uh. Had a full schedule this morning and Carlita didn't show up—morning sickness, she says." RaeJean lowered her voice to a stage whisper. "I figure she decided to sleep late and go off for the day with that fool husband of hers. Ain't two ways about it, that girl is on her last chance at the Snip and Curl."

"I think," Kristin murmured, hiding a smile at the reverent tone RaeJean always used for the name of her shop, "that you were saying the same thing when I was in town for my daddy's funeral going on two years ago."

Her hands on her ample hips, RaeJean snorted. "Meant it then, and I mean it now." Behind her, a timer buzzed, but she waved away the sound as if it were an annoying fly and fixed a stern eye on Kristin's shoulder-length hair. "Now, what can I do for you? You need a cut? Some style?" She reached out and ran a hand through Kristin's silky, straight strands that had defied a lifetime of effort to add curls, waves and even the tidiness of a smooth chignon. "A good perm and some color would brighten you right up. Need something more lively than just strawberry blond, I think."

Cody's eyes widened with obvious fascination as he came back in with a Coke and glanced between RaeJean's bouffant, Technicolor Big Texas Hair, and Kristin's own simple style.

"Um…not today. You're really busy, and I need to run." When RaeJean's appraisal didn't waiver, Kristin took a step back. "And I'm just a wash-and-wear sort of girl. Really."

RaeJean cocked her head. "Was there something else? You need help out at that place of yours?" Her face brightened. "I'd be happy to give you some decorating advice. Curtains—wallpaper—you name it."

Cody sidled next to Kristin and tugged anxiously on the back of her shirt, undoubtedly envisioning flamingos and ruffles at their rustic place in the country.

"I think we're set on that score, but thanks for the offer." Behind her, a silver bell tinkled over the door and someone stepped inside. Over her aunt's shoulder, Kristin saw one of the customers impatiently drumming her fingernails on the arm of her dryer chair. "I do need to talk to you, though. I've tried and tried to reach Aunt Nora, but she doesn't answer her phone, and I'm just afraid…" She glanced down at Cody. "Well, I just need to talk to her before she does anything…big."

RaeJean nodded decisively, snagged Kristin's arm and hauled her forward. "Family first, I always say. You two sit here for just a minute. I need to do a fast comb-out, turn off that dryer, and I'll be back." She smiled at the newcomer. "Ruth, just set yourself down and have a cup of coffee. You're a mite early, anyway."

RaeJean bustled away, checked each head of hair under a dryer, and scurried back to the woman sitting in one of the styling chairs.

Kristin hovered at the entryway for a moment.

"C'mon, Mom. Let's *go*." Cody begged. "The first football practice starts in an hour!"

"And it's just on the edge of town. This won't take long, I promise." She gave his shoulder a reassuring squeeze, then smothered a sigh as she sank into one of the pink plastic chairs in the tiny waiting area. Cody stubbornly stood at the door, his lower lip jutting out and his hands jammed in his pockets.

The diminutive woman at the door strolled to the back of the shop and returned with two cups of coffee, handed one to Kristin and settled her thin frame into a chair in the corner. She tipped her head toward the ledge under the window facing the street. "There's cream and sugar packets over there in the pink basket."

"Thanks. Black is fine."

The woman chuckled. "You might change your mind. RaeJeans's coffee could eat rust off a truck, but leastways it's hot."

Kristin took in her pale skin and faded, silver-streaked blond hair. There was a sharp, observant glint in her eyes as she curved a bony hand around her coffee cup for a quick sip and studied Kristin over the rim. She seemed vaguely familiar, though Kristin couldn't place her.

The woman cocked her head, as if she, too, were trying to remember, then she sat back in her chair with a satisfied smile. "I'm Ruth Holden. My husband is the rector at St. Mark's Episcopal." She pursed her lips. "I'll bet you've come here for the land giveaway."

Kristin laughed. "Good guess."

"I've been on the Home Free Committee since last fall, and we've already had some nice young families move into the area. I think I must've seen your photo in that first batch of applications. In fact, I'll bet you're—" she pursed her lips for a moment, apparently searching her memory "—Kristin and Cody Peters?"

She leaned forward and offered her hand. "My husband had a light stroke last spring and was hospitalized in Austin for several weeks, so I wasn't at your interview."

"I hope he's doing well."

"He's a strong man, determined as can be. He was back in the pulpit within three weeks after coming home." Ruth's voice filled with pride. "For over forty years, nothing has mattered to him more than the moral welfare of his flock."

Settling back into her chair, Ruth took another sip of her coffee. "I want you to know how pleased the Committee is to see all of you young folks moving into town. Just this month, we brought in a husband and wife who are teachers, a young fellow with a new degree in nursing, and a family planning to raise goats and sheep on fifty acres west of town. You must be the physician's assistant who'll be running the local health clinic."

Despite occasional visits to Homestead to see her father over the years, the easy familiarity of the small town still caught Kristin unawares. In Dallas and Austin, she'd barely known her neighbors, and people had rarely stopped to chat.

She nodded. "The land deal is a wonderful opportunity. We're not actually both the Peters, though. Cody kept his father's last name after my divorce, but last summer I finally decided to go back to my maiden name. Cantrell."

"Divorced?" Ruth blinked, her mouth work-

ing. She visibly drew back into herself. "But I thought…"

"I'm sure it was clear on my application."

Ruth brought her hand up to her mouth. "A-and you said *Cantrell?*"

"That's right." Kristin rose and caught Cody's hand. "My dad was Nate Cantrell."

Her brow furrowed, Ruth looked from the boy to Kristin. *So it was happening again.* That flash of recognition, the moment of prejudgment.

Maybe it hadn't been such a good idea to come back here, after all.

"I should have *recognized* you," Ruth said faintly.

"I was just ten when I left with my mom. When I came to see my dad, he was usually out working on one ranch or another, and we rarely ever made the long trip into town."

"I see. It isn't…I mean…" Her cheeks flushed pink. "It's just…"

Mindful of Cody's heightened interest in the conversation, Kristin gave his hand a quick squeeze. "I think we'd better get moving, Tiger, so we aren't late for that practice. I'll just try calling RaeJean later."

At the door, she urged him outside, and then turned back toward the flustered woman. "I'm sorry if I've upset you."

"No…I mean, yes…" The color in the older woman's cheeks betrayed her struggle for tact.

"Whatever you may have thought about him, I do know my father had a good heart." Kristin held the woman's gaze. "I'm here because I'm good at what I do, this town needs me, and because I need a new start for my son. My last name should make no difference at all."

Ruth's mouth tightened. "You misunderstand me, dear. There are people who still blame your father for how things changed around here. They might not be so ready to forgive."

"IT'S GOOD TO HAVE YOU back in Texas, son." Leland Havens clapped Ryan on the shoulder, then winced in sympathy as Ryan flinched. "Sorry. I didn't think. How're you doing, now? Better?"

"Fine." Ignoring the pain radiating down his arm, Ryan took a step back and hooked his thumbs in the front pockets of his Levi's.

The years had been kinder to Clint than they'd been to his lifelong friend. Deep creases lined Leland's cheeks, his hair had thinned to a few long wisps on top. His once imposing, elegant frame no longer stood quite as tall. The man had been Ryan's boyhood mentor, and had once seemed as ageless as the massive live oaks lining the drive. Now, surely in his late sixties, he'd aged beyond his years and his mortality was all too apparent.

"I'm glad you could drop in so soon. I imagine a young buck like you would rather spend a Saturday morning on horseback or out on a golf course, eh?"

He waved Ryan to a chair in the corner of his office, motioned to his secretary from the open doorway, and then sat next to Ryan. "I suppose Garrett hightailed it off to some rodeo for the weekend?"

"He left late Wednesday for Billings." Without so much as a fast hello and goodbye for the eldest brother he'd once followed around like an orphan pup.

Leland eyed Ryan thoughtfully. "Nothing his daddy says gets through to him. He's heading for a full-body cast if he doesn't quit chasin' bulls and gold buckles every weekend."

"And the little buckle bunnies, from what Trevor says. I understand Garrett's been busy leaving a trail of broken hearts from Canada to Houston."

"I keep warning him to be careful. All we need is one avaricious gal who knows the Gallagher name, and the potential for bad press shoots to the moon."

A valid concern, Ryan supposed. With that deep-dimpled, aw-shucks grin and devilish twinkle in his eye, Garrett had always been a charmer.

He'd usually gotten exactly what he wanted while making others feel happy to hand it over.

"At least Trevor is well settled," Leland continued. "Nice wife, kids."

"And works his tail off, from what I've seen so far."

Leland took a pair of half reading glasses from the breast pocket of his coat, settled them low on his nose, then studied Ryan over the rim. "He's a good hands-on manager. He knows cattle, horses, people."

"But...?" Ryan raised a brow.

"He doesn't have the skills or the foresight to handle the broader picture. We just need to get past the Nate Cantrell incident, put the ranch affairs back in order and hire a permanent manager."

"Well, my skills aren't exactly current, unless Dad needs a sniper with an M4 guarding the ranch."

A portly secretary dressed in a severe black skirt and jacket marched in with a tray of coffee cups and a small coffeepot. After settling the tray on the end table between them, she bustled out, closing the door firmly behind her.

Leland leaned forward to hand Ryan a cup, then cradled the other one in both hands and smiled at him affectionately. "Your brothers wanted you here, so look at this as a chance to rest up, after all you've been through." He paused. "You've given enough of your life to the service. With your business degree, you could head for Chicago or New York, if you want something besides cedars, sand and sagebrush in your backyard."

"I'm still on active duty. I plan to go back as soon as I can."

Leland's sympathetic gaze drifted to Ryan's knee as he put his cup down. "Maybe you'd like to, but—"

Ryan struggled to curb his irritation. "After surgeries and rehab, they're even able to return some amputees to the front lines. I'll go back, even if I have to be an instructor."

"Of course, of course." Leland lifted his hands in a placating gesture. "Forgive me."

Ryan winced. Leland had always kept the best interests of the Gallaghers at heart, and he certainly didn't deserve to be on the receiving end of Ryan's unpredictable bitterness. "No…the apology should be mine."

Clasping his hands loosely in his lap, Leland leaned back and gave Ryan a fatherly smile. "That time when you got your first Purple Heart, a few years ago? There was mention of it at a high school graduation assembly. After that, at least five elementary classrooms started sending letters and gift boxes to servicemen overseas." He shook his head in wonderment. "Townsfolk filled those collection boxes to overflowing."

Surprised and a little embarrassed, Ryan looked away. "At least some good came out of it. I didn't realize anyone even knew."

Leland laughed. "Then you probably don't remember the Niebauers, who run the *Herald*. Millicent isn't bigger than a minute, but she's got a nose for news and the tenacity of a bulldog. Though, come to think of it, she didn't get wind of your injuries a few months ago. Just the Purple Heart."

"So how bad are things out at the ranch—really?"

"Really?" He shook his head slowly. "Up until a few years ago, your father watched over both his political career and the ranch with a sharp eye. Nothing got past that man—*nothing*. Then his vision started failing, but of course being Clint, he never let on. We know Nate got away with at least sixty grand, but the books are such a mess that it could be double that, easily."

"Pretty much what Trevor said…and what I found in the forensic accountant's report."

"Clint may be snarling about your arrival, but I'm sure he's angrier at himself than he is at anyone else. Once he simmers down, he'll be grateful."

"So I'm just supposed to reorganize the bookkeeping system?" Ryan sighed. "That's something a good office manager would do."

"Not with Clint bird-dogging every last step of the way…and it's not just the bookkeeping, either. You could revamp the hunting lease program, and maybe work on marketing angles that will get it moving. The quarter horse and beef cattle programs probably need some work, as well." Leland grabbed a legal pad on his desk, ran a forefinger down a list of notes, then set the pad back down. "Whatever you can do while you're here will help the new manager who follows you. I'll assist in any way I can."

"And the missing money?"

"Honestly, it's a lost cause." Leland splayed his fingers on his thighs. "But if you come across *anything*—any clues whatsoever—let me know immediately. I'll get the private investigator on it right away." Leland studied Ryan over the rim of his glasses again. "The corporation needs that money back, but this situation can't get out to the press or the sheriff's office—either way, news will spread. Clint's political rivals would have a heyday crowing about him 'allowing' his own business to end up in such disarray. This next election will likely be his last, and there are still issues that mean a great deal to him."

"Right." Ryan shifted in his chair, wishing he'd taken a couple Tylenol before leaving the ranch.

"After all this time, the horses are out of the barn, anyway."

"The loss came at a bad time. Remember the K-Bar-C?"

"The Braxton place. Shares part of our eastern property line."

"Place went up for auction twelve years ago. A group of locals formed a consortium, bought it and also picked up some smaller properties to create KC Enterprises. Every one of those investors had dreams of making big money. Some of them poured their life savings into the deal, some mortgaged their own property to scrape enough money together."

The K-Bar-C... "Trevor filled me in on some of this already, and I do know Dad and Braxton weren't the best of friends," Ryan mused. "Clyde's place was upstream on the aquifer that supplies the Four Aces, and I vaguely remember Dad ranting about water rights."

"Which is why he wanted to buy out Braxton for years. We put together one offer after another, but Braxton hung on to it until he died in his late 80s—out of sheer spite, Clint figured. The heirs scrabbled over the estate and ultimately ran it into bankruptcy. It came up for auction when I was out East for a couple months and your dad was in the middle of some big tussle in the State Senate. It sold to a group of locals."

"I can imagine how happy he was when he heard the news too late."

"You have no idea," Leland retorted. "Then just a year ago, the consortium folded. Crazy idea anyway, if you ask me. Drought hit. Cattle prices were down. The partners were up to their ears in debt and way behind on taxes."

"So Dad—"

"This time he knew about it. But he was cash poor, especially after so much money was embezzled. He couldn't pull a down payment together quick enough, and the town council foreclosed on the property. They're using it for that homesteader program, bringing in more families to grow the town. Your father is still furious, and he's had nearly a year to adjust."

"Homesteads?"

"At very low-cost loans that mostly just cover the back taxes, with no down payment. If all goes according to plan, there'll be hundreds of families sitting on top of that aquifer, drawing water away." Leland pursed his lips. "The sheriff is on the Home Free committee, along with Frances Haase, the town librarian, Father Holden's wife, mayor Miranda Wright and Enfield."

"Enfield. I can imagine what Dad thinks about that."

Leland pushed himself to his feet and started to pace. "Local politics are small potatoes to your father, of course, but those two have been rivals since they were kids. He probably thinks the entire land giveaway deal was Arlen's scheme to irritate him. It wasn't, though. Miranda came up with the idea and sold everyone else on it."

"I was out riding yesterday and ran across a boy in our east pasture. I figured his family was just renting the old Cedar Grove place."

"Nope. You just met your neighbors. Permanent neighbors, that is. There'll be a lot more coming. And a lot of the property adjoins the Four Aces."

"The boy was Kris Cantrell's son."

Leland's jaw dropped. "She's back? Does your father know?"

"That Nate's daughter is in town? Yes. That she's a neighbor? I have no idea. I suppose there's been some sort of notice in the local papers about the homestead awards, but he spends a lot of time in Austin."

Leland whistled. "Well don't that just beat all."

"I don't think she was any happier about seeing me that I was to see her."

A muscle ticked in his jaw as Leland drummed his fingers on his thigh. "I know you two were close once. She was a pretty little thing, but Clint said she was bad news."

How much had Dad told him, all those years ago?

"I'm old enough to take care of myself, this time around," Ryan shot back.

Once burned, twice shy, his mother had said more than once over the years, and she was right. He wouldn't make the same mistake twice.

CHAPTER FIVE

"MOM, LOOK! HORSES!" Cody struggled to lean forward despite the shoulder strap of his seat belt.

"I...see." Shielding her eyes from the noon sun, Kristin parked in front of their house, stepped out of her red pickup and stared at a grizzled old Mexican—one who was all-too familiar—unloading a pale buckskin from a battered old horse trailer.

On the other side of the trailer, she could see just the hindquarters of a sorrel standing slant-hipped, its tail flicking lazily.

And sure enough, a wizened figure in dusty boots and an old gray Stetson soon rounded the back of the trailer. "Howdy," she barked as she slammed the trailer gate shut with a resounding clang. "I was fixin' to leave you a note if you didn't show up in time."

"Show up?" Kristin said faintly. "In *time?*"

Cody took off running and skidded to a stop just a few yards from the horses. "Wow! Are these for us? You really did get me a *horse?*"

Kristin hurried to catch up, grabbing his shoulder before he got any closer. "Aunt Nora—"

With a dismissive wave, Nora retrieved the horse tied to the other side of the trailer, motioned to Luis, her ranch hand, and, with Kristin and Cody tagging along behind, put the horses into the corral by the barn.

Cody was clearly thrilled. Kristin felt... stunned.

"Cool! Can we ride now? Which one is mine?" Cody launched himself up onto the split rail fence and hooked his elbows over the top. "Can I have the tan one?"

"Buckskin, son. Boots is a buckskin. I figure you'd best ride Rebel, the sorrel. He's been around the world with kids on his back. No surprises with that'n." Nora tipped her hat back with a forefinger and studied him. Her sun-cured skin baked to a leathery brown after a lifetime outside in the blazing heat of Texas, she was sixty-three but had looked much older than that for the past twenty years. "Did your momma teach you how to ride, yet?"

His eyes veered away from the horses and met Kristin's for just an instant. "Sorta."

Kristin, her head reeling, gathered her thoughts. "I think there's been a mistake. We're not really ready for this, and I'm not sure I can afford—"

"Pshaw!" Nora snorted. "What would your

daddy say, you coming back here with your boy and not putting some horses in your barn? You were on Teacup before you could walk."

Remembering her first ancient, arthritic pony, Kristin couldn't help but smile. "True. But right now, money's tight, and I haven't checked the fencing, and I just don't think—"

"Mo-om!" Cody cried, looking between her and Nora. "She's gonna let us have 'em. Pleeeaasse?"

Nora leveled a long look at Kristin, then slowly shook her head in disgust. "RaeJean didn't tell you. I swear she doesn't have the sense of a cactus. I figured she'd see you around town, and she was supposed to tell you I was coming over one of these first days."

RaeJean *was* a little absentminded, but at the thought of causing additional friction between her late father's sisters—who tended to bicker anyway— Kristin scrambled for the right thing to say. "I went to see her yesterday, but she was busy, then we left and I just forgot to call her later. My fault, really. Totally mine."

Nora harrumphed and exchanged glances with Luis. "I suppose…we could take these two horses home."

"Mom, please!" Cody jumped off the fence and ran to grab Kristin's hand. "I'll do the chores. I'll do everything, honest. They won't cost much—

there's nice pasture, and we already have the barn."

Kristin held back a sigh. "What's the story on these geldings?"

Luis chuckled. "Your aunt, she did a favor for these fine boys. They belong to this place, but couldn't stay without someone here."

"They *belong* here?" Mystified, Kristin studied the horses through the rails of the fence. If not registered quarter horses they were certainly the type, with broad, muscular hindquarters and powerful chests.

"Foaled on this very property, ten years ago," Nora said briskly. "This piece once belonged to an old cowboy who'd saved up enough to retire on a little place of his own." The note of affection in her voice suggested that they might have been friends. "Jim broke these boys out nice and gentle, rode most every day. Two years ago his heart gave out. Had no relatives, so the sheriff asked if I'd take the horses and his dog. The land was bought out by the K-Bar-C investors."

"There's a dog?" Cody scanned the yard. "Did you bring him, too?"

"Ole Scout is probably asleep under the tractor back home. I don't know that he's up to any more changes." Nora pursed her lips, considering. "But if you're looking for a dog, too—"

"Yes!"

"No," Kristin said quickly. "Not right now, anyway. And about the horses—I just don't have the money right now to buy them, much less for the shoer and vet and feed."

Crossing her arms, Nora looked exasperated. "Missy, you're getting them for *free.* You got twenty acres here, with some good grassy bottom ground. They're both easy keepers, and they've been barefoot from day one. You know as well as I do that you can do your own paste worming and vaccinations."

"I don't have any friends here. Just think how cool it would be for you and me to go riding, Mom," Cody pleaded. *"Please?* I'll… I'll do dishes forever. I'll…I'll do anything you say."

A smile played at the corners of Luis's mouth. "Sounds like your young caballero is in great need of a good horse," he mused. "Maybe you could just give this a try. If it don't work out, we come get the horses. Eh, Nora?"

Nora nodded decisively. "Done."

"I got my fence pliers in the truck," Luis added, giving Cody a wink. "You and me can ride the property line right now, make sure the fence is tight."

"Yes!" Cody pumped his fist and tackled Kristin around the waist. "Thanks, Mom!"

Dazed, she returned his hug, then spread her

hands palms up as she met Nora's amused gaze. "But the tack—I don't have anything."

Nora hiked a thumb toward the back of the pickup. "Figured as much. We tossed in a coupla old roping saddles, bridles and some other equipment. It all came from Jim's barn anyway, so it's only right it comes back here. I've got no need for it."

Within minutes, the horses were saddled and Cody, trembling with excitement, was aboard Rebel. Tipping his hat, Luis started into the pasture with Cody close behind.

Kristin watched them disappear over the hill, then turned to Nora and gave her a hug. "Thank you. It was really sweet of you to do this."

Flustered, Nora took an awkward step back. "Needed to do this for my friend Jim," she said, her voice rough. "Nothing more than that."

The unexpected hint at a softer side touched Kristin. Nora had always been the loner of the two aunts—a proud, independent woman who'd managed a ranch on her own since her early twenties. Kristin chose her words carefully. "Of course. I know he'd be thankful for everything you've done. I promise I'll take good care of this place, and his horses, too."

Nora turned away and busied herself with gathering the halters, lead ropes and hoof picks that Luis and Cody had left on the fenders of the trailer. "You be careful, hear? Young woman and a child out here, all alone…"

"I'm not some city slicker afraid of the dark, Aunt Nora. Remember, I spent part of my childhood here. I won't miss the streetlights and traffic."

"It's not just that." Nora inclined her head toward the barn, so Kristin fell in step with her as she headed that way.

Once the tack was stowed, Nora leaned against a stall door with one booted foot cocked back to rest on the rough timber. "I don't know how much you know about your dad." She laughed dryly. "Kids usually aren't aware of everything that's going on, and I expect your momma didn't feel too inclined to share a lot of good memories, eh?"

"True," Kristin admitted. "Though she didn't run him down in front of me. I know they fought a lot more after the foreclosure of our ranch. And after the divorce, I didn't get to see him much." She forced a smile. "I missed him."

"My brother was a good man. A hard worker, and I believe he was as honest as they come. Things never did go right for him, though. Drought and cattle prices foreclosed his ranch. He scraped and saved, and rallied a lot of friends to join him in a partnership to buy thousands of acres of good Texas Hill Country, back before the prices hiked up so high. People…" Nora paused.

"Well, when the consortium went under, there were a lot of people around here who were hurt bad. Some lost their life savings, some lost the family ranches they'd mortgaged to join in. A lot of them blamed your dad, saying he'd talked them into a foolish scheme."

"But it wasn't his fault, right?"

"No. It wasn't the fault of the man who oversaw the day-to-day operation of the place, either. Zeb Ritter worked hard as any man could, and your dad was out there, too, working twelve-to eighteen-hour days for him. The economy and the drought were at fault, but it's easier to take failure when you can pin it on someone."

Maybe that's why her dad hadn't had much time for a young daughter who'd lived so far away. "That's not *fair.*"

"Yeah, well, Zeb committed suicide almost eighteen months ago, and your dad died the month before. Neither one is left to blame, now." Nora's lips thinned. "I wanted you to understand, because there are still some locals with hard feelings."

"I've already run into a few of them."

"There's something else." Nora paced to the side door of the barn and stared out over the dry, rolling landscape with her thumbs hooked in the back pockets of her worn Levi's. "Everyone in these parts knows how that sorry excuse-of-a-man

Gallagher wanted the K-Bar-C land. Power and control is everything to him, and it sticks in his craw that the Home Free committee nabbed it."

Kristin joined her at the doorway. "But what can he do about it?"

"Nothing legal," Nora scoffed. "I just want you to understand what's going on around here, and I want you to be careful."

"I hardly think the man can kick me off my land."

Nora rested a calloused hand on Kristin's arm. "Your dad worked for Clint up until a few weeks before he died. They must've had a big argument, because Nate either quit or was fired. I'll go to my grave thinking there was something fishy about my brother's death so soon after that."

Startled, Kristin drew in a sharp breath. "But it was ruled an accident."

"I have no proof. But your dad drove that road most every day of his life. He knew every curve, every bump. The weather was dry. The sun had just set, so the light was still good. The sheriff doesn't agree with me, but I believe someone forced your dad's truck off the road. And I think I know who it was."

ON TUESDAY MORNING, Kristin's stomach tightened when she checked the time. Eight o'clock.

By eight-thirty she felt as if tumbleweed had lodged in her throat.

She nearly jumped out of her skin when the clinic phone rang. It was a wrong number, though in small-town fashion, the caller managed to stretch that inadvertent call into a good ten minutes about local gossip and the weather.

By a quarter of ten, the waiting room was still empty and Kristin breathed a sigh of relief...until a moment later, when she heard heavy footsteps tromping up the steps and the front door of the clinic squealed open.

Ryan walked in, his face a grim mask. "Sorry we're late."

Senator Gallagher followed him, leveled a cold look at Kristin, and folded his arms. "I have a cardiologist in Austin."

"But you haven't seen him in almost two years, and *he's over an hour away,*" Ryan said evenly. The set of his jaw suggested that the trip into town hadn't been easy. "You need a local doctor, too."

"Come on back, Senator. This won't take long." Facing the man who'd nearly destroyed her years ago, Kristin dredged up a weak smile. *I believe someone forced your dad's truck off the road—and I think I know who it was.* Though Nora had refused to elaborate, it didn't take much imagination to guess who that someone was she referred to.

When she was younger, Kristin had discovered

just how cruel and domineering Clint could be...
yet it hardly seemed plausible that an influential
senator would jeopardize his privileged status
with murder.

"We have some old records from the Dr. Grady
days, but I'm sure we'll need to update your history, sir. We'll also need a release so we can get
copies of your current records in Austin."

Ryan turned to look out the window of the
clinic as Kristin led his father down the hall to
an exam room. Clint took a chair in the corner
instead of the edge of the exam table, his face
impassive.

His responses to her questions were cursory at
best—and likely not entirely accurate, given the
stubborn jut of his jaw. Fortunately, he signed a
release for the transfer of his medical records in
Austin. While he was disrobing, she sent it to the
cardiology clinic and then called them to ask if
she could get the records ASAP.

Back in the exam room, she found Clint sitting
on the exam table, his shirt off. He sat in silence as
she took his blood pressure both sitting and standing, then listened to his heart and lungs. "You said
you weren't on any medications. Is that correct?"

His mouth tightened. "Nothing I need to take."

"I'm hearing some PVCs—an irregular beat. I'd
like to do an EKG while you're here." When he
bristled, she added, "It's apparently been a while

since you've been to a doctor, so it's good to have a baseline."

"Who reads it, *you?*"

His derisive tone rankled. "Yes, and then I'll send it on to Dr. Hernandez and the cardiologist in San Antonio."

She rolled the EKG machine from its place in the corner and attached the leads, then ran a tape on him, watching the needle trace a telltale pattern that confirmed her initial diagnosis.

He apparently noticed something in her expression, because his eyebrows drew together. "Normal, I suppose."

"Not entirely," she hedged. "Though in a man your age we can hardly expect a twenty-year-old heart, right? We'll have a report back from the cardiologist by tomorrow, and we should have your old records by then, too."

He looked wary as she prepared to draw blood samples. "Are you okay with this? Do you want to lie down?"

"No," he growled. "Let's just get this farce over with."

She bit back the impulse to defend her training and experience as she applied the tourniquet, swiftly found a good vein and drew two test tubes. He turned slightly ashen, and his skin felt damp by the time she finished.

When he started to climb off the table, she held

him gently back. "Do needles bother you? Maybe you'd better sit for just a minute. You're a little pale."

He jerked his arm away. "I don't need your advice, missy. Now leave me be so I can dress."

She lingered close by, anyway, as he stood, wavered a little, then seemed to regain his color. "I'll go on out to the front desk and see if your records have come yet."

She'd gathered her lab tray and was almost to the door when he barked her name. "Yes?"

He'd shrugged into his shirt and was starting to do up the first button, but his gaze was pinned on her face with an intensity that made her shiver.

"I don't know why you're back in town, and I don't much care. But you keep away from my son, you hear?"

CHAPTER SIX

DR. HERNANDEZ HAD PROMISED that a nurse would arrive the Tuesday after Labor Day weekend. She hadn't mentioned that he'd be balding and burly, with a massive tattoo of an 18-wheeler on his left upper arm and a gold-capped front tooth.

"I'm Max Zimmerman." He shook Kristin's hand with enough force to make her wince, his eyes sparkling behind trendy wire rims at odds with the rest of his well-aged biker image. "Boy, howdy. Thought I'd never get here today. Dr. Lou did my health exam, blood work and TB-tine at the main clinic this morning, and then I must've watched six orientation videos. I'm still on a caffeine high from trying to stay awake."

Kristin had been in a dark mood since Clint and Ryan left a few hours earlier, but now she grinned at Max. "It's great having you aboard."

He followed her second glance to his truck tattoo and smiled ruefully. "My clinic jacket will cover it. I got a little wild in my days after the service, and unfortunately wasn't content with a simple 'Mom.'"

Though he had that, too, along with a heart and the name Rosalie on his other muscular forearm.

She gave him a tour of the building, ending up at the front desk where she offered him a seat and pulled up an extra chair for herself. "You and I will be on our own for a while, until things pick up. I understand that, for now, you'll handle the phone. We'll make sure the insurance and billing forms are complete, but they're computerized and bookkeepers at the main clinic will handle them."

"Good deal." He opened the appointment book with obvious relish and flipped through some of the pages. His face fell. "There's hardly anyone in here."

"Today is our first day. Doc Grady died a few years back, so it might take a while. There'll be notices in the *Homestead Herald* and some of the papers in the surrounding towns."

"And the town should grow, with the Home Free homesteading program. I understand you and I are both part of it…though I didn't fit the preferred family profile." His smile didn't quite reach his eyes. "Still, I had nursing skills to offer, and I'll have a small-engine repair business on the side. They gave me a house at the end of Pecan Street, with a shop building in back."

"How long have you been in nursing?"

"I was a medic in the service for a few years. I wanted to go to college afterward, but just couldn't hack it given some of the stuff I was still dealing with. Nightmares, flashbacks—you know the drill. I ended up driving a truck for a while."

Kristin tipped her head in silent acknowledgment of all he'd gone through. "What made you change jobs?"

"After my wife died, I went back to school. Seeing what those nurses did for her made me want to give back something, you know? They made all the difference."

The pain in his voice sounded so fresh that she wanted to give him a hug. "I'm sorry about your loss."

"I miss her every day." He flipped back to the current date in the appointment book. "I see you had a patient this morning. How'd that go?"

"Not the best start."

He gave the name a second glance, then looked up at her in surprise. "Clint Gallagher. The state *senator*?"

"One and the same. His son made him come, but he wasn't happy about it. He seems to be in denial regarding his health and hasn't been compliant with medical advice." She nudged Clint's patient file with a forefinger. "His old medical records just came from Austin. Hyperlipidemia, with a cholesterol of 325 and elevated triglycerides of 550. A history of angina, with a few E.R.

visits. He was started on a beta blocker, Lipitor and aspirin therapy two years ago, but he's never followed through. Today's EKG showed occasional PVCs."

Max whistled under his breath. "A walking heart attack."

"And he's not going to listen to me, either. He made that clear enough today. His family and mine have some…history, so Dr. Lou will probably have to talk to him."

"He'd better get over it. She isn't here that often, and in an emergency he'll have to see you anyway, the fool."

Max's disgust made Kristin laugh. "I think he'd have to be unconscious."

"Sounds like quite a guy. Now he'll have to deal with a female doctor, a P.A. he dislikes and a tattooed ex-trucker. He'll probably decide he's safer at the vet."

CODY STOOD on the sidelines with his fists clenched, watching the other fourth grade boys gather around the football coach. He'd been given a time-out for the last half of the practice just because stupid Ricky Garner was a big fat baby. *It wasn't fair. It wasn't, wasn't fair.*

And now, because he couldn't walk home like most of the other kids, he had to wait here for Mom…and she was at work, so she might be late.

Fighting back tears, he blinked hard and watched the coach—one of the fourth grade teachers—clap Hayden Gallagher on the back.

At the edge of the schoolyard, a bunch of dads leaned against the hoods of their pickups. They'd been there the whole time, cheering and shouting, as if they were watching the Dallas Cowboys instead of some stupid grade school practice, where hardly anyone caught the ball and some of the kids cried if they got tackled just a little too hard.

"Come on over here, Cody," the coach called out. "You need to hear this, too."

A surge of rebellion made him want to stand still, but somehow his feet started moving. A couple of the kids snickered and elbowed each other when he reached the group, and he felt his face heat.

"…so tomorrow, be here right after school. We have enough boys so we can divide into two teams for practice. Got that? Three-thirty sharp, in uniform. And remind your parents, because we don't always meet on Thursdays."

The town boys raced for their bicycles. Others headed for their dads in the parking lot. Cody kicked at a clump of dry grass as he watched them go. Hayden's dad came out onto the grass to meet his son halfway and—oh, boy—so did the neighbor guy who'd given Cody a ride on his horse last Friday night. Ryan somebody.

Jealousy burned through Cody. How fair was that? He had a dad, too, but he lived in Dallas and never found much time to visit. And when he did…

A single tear burned down Cody's cheek, so he turned his back and angrily rubbed it away with the back of his hand, glad everyone was too far away to see.

"Hey, son, do you have a ride home?" The voice was deep and familiar, and Cody turned to find Ryan standing by the open door of a silver pickup. "Do you need to use my cell phone?"

The guy was *sooo* cool. Hayden had taken over Show and Tell for three days running, blabbing on and on about his uncle who went on secret missions for the army and had been badly hurt. Just having Ryan notice him made Cody feel warm inside, but out of the corner of his eye he could see Mom's pickup coming down the street. "Nah, my mom's here."

Ryan looked up the street. "Is that her?"

Cody nodded, wishing she hadn't showed up so soon.

"You did a great job at practice today. Keep it up." He got in his truck and shut the door, but didn't drive off until Mom's truck pulled to a stop and Cody climbed in.

"Howdy, Tiger." Mom reached over to give him a one-armed hug, then put the truck in gear and drove out of the parking lot. "Did you have a good time?"

Embarrassed by the hug, even though no other guys were around, Cody peered out the window and watched the silver pickup disappear.

Football wasn't about having a good time. It was about being one of the guys, and trying superhard, and doing something better than you ever thought you could, so people would cheer and say you were great. It was about dads giving bear hugs and *way-to-go!* punches on a guy's arm. It was about a lot of things Cody would never have, because he already knew he was awkward and slow…and his dad thought sports were boring.

"Why doesn't Dad visit us?"

Mom glanced at him before she turned out onto the highway. "You saw him not too long ago—just a couple weeks before we moved."

Cody picked at a ketchup stain on his jeans.

"Remember?" she coaxed. "You were there for the whole weekend, and he took you out for pizza."

Where Dad had complained about the waiting line, the slow service and the pizza itself…and had grumbled the entire time about wanting to just walk out of the place. Back at his condo, his new wife, Darla, had kept frowning at Cody as if he might get things dirty if he even breathed. "Yeah, I remember."

"You know how busy he is—he has a very important job at that bank, and he helps a lot of people. He'll still come to see you, though, and I know you'll get to visit him, too." Mom gave Cody a teasing smile. "Why so glum? You've got someone named Rebel waiting for you, and that sure wouldn't have happened in the city."

"Can we ride tonight?"

"You bet. If you do your homework while I make supper, we'll have plenty of daylight left. And I know just the place I'd like to go."

RYAN PULLED TO A STOP on the crest of the hill overlooking the Four Aces. Below him lay white-fenced corrals, horse barns and loafing sheds, and farther on, the cattle pens. On another gentle rise, the sprawling brick house that had once been his home.

It sure didn't feel like home anymore, though, and after a week of living under that roof, he figured he'd be happier just about anywhere else.

Trevor put in twelve-hour days as the foreman, then went home to his wife and family. Garrett still hadn't shown up after his last rodeo...and after supper, Adelfa retired to her own apartment at the back of the main house. Mom had been living in Dallas for years.

That left only Clint, who holed up in his office until nearly midnight working on his upcoming reelection campaign and fielding countless phone calls that came in on his private office line.

The house felt hollow, echoing with memories. It offered far too much solitude now. Too much time to think. To second-guess.

And to mourn.

Shaking off his melancholy thoughts, he promptly ended up with yet another—Kristin. Leland had suggested that Kristin might have received some embezzled money from her father, but that sure didn't seem plausible.

She was homesteading a rundown house in the middle of nowhere. She drove a rusted truck and mostly wore old T-shirts and jeans. There hadn't been any evidence of new bikes or expensive toys for Cody at that place, and Ryan had a feeling that if anyone enjoyed nicer things in that family, it would be him.

Kristin's boy. According to Trevor, Cody was in Hayden's class at school, but the similarity pretty much ended there.

Hayden was a handful. Wild and exuberant, he was always looking for adventure, his eyes full of mischief and a fast comeback ready at any time.

Standing out on the field alone this afternoon, his chin raised at a belligerent angle and his hands jammed in his pockets, Cody looked like the loneliest kid Ryan had ever seen. There was anger in him, too, and defiance…yet he'd seemed almost pathetically grateful when Ryan had offered the use of his cell phone. What was going on there?

Abuse came to mind. But Kristin had never seemed the type, and there didn't seem to be a dad in the picture anymore.

Ryan felt a twinge of anger. She'd kicked him aside like a pile of dirty laundry when she learned that he wouldn't inherit any part of the ranch. After that, Kristin had gone after the first rich boy she met. And apparently that hadn't lasted, either.

And now the one who was suffering was that young boy.

The children…it was always the children who suffered most. He closed his eyes against the images from the Middle East that still haunted his nights, but he couldn't block the sounds. The screams. Bowing his head, he immersed himself in the guilt and the horror of it all. There was nothing he could do to change things. Nothing he could do to bring them back.

All he could do was remember…and remember. Until the day he died.

The roar of a truck shook him out of his private memorial. In the rearview mirror he saw a cloud of dust boiling skyward behind a pickup that had to be doing nearly seventy on a gravel road.

He threw his truck into gear and pulled way over to the side, hoping the driver didn't lose control at the crest of the hill. Seconds later, gravel hit the side of his truck like a barrage of buckshot as the vehicle thundered by.

Ryan followed the other driver home and parked next to him. He was out of his truck and at the other driver's door as the guy stepped out. "I hope there was a fire," he snapped. "You could've killed someone driving like that."

The man hoisted a bull rope onto his shoulder, turned and gave him an arrogant grin. *Garrett.* "Just clockin' good time out of town. Most people are smart enough to get out of my way."

Ryan's anger blazed. "But everyone deserves to live, punk. You're just too dumb to realize it."

Garrett tipped back his head and laughed, his brash cockiness unfazed. "Well, aren't we lucky. The big hero is back. I can't wait to see what happens around here now."

CHAPTER SEVEN

IF SHE WAS EVER going to find out the truth about her dad, she'd have to start asking the right people in town, which meant she'd have to get closer to the Gallaghers. Clint's hostility had only firmed her resolve.

Tomorrow, she would stop in at the sheriff's office, and this evening, she and Cody were going for a nice ride…in the right direction.

When they reached the end of their pasture, she twisted in her saddle and rested a palm on Boots's broad rump. A rusted pipe gate led into the vast, deserted reaches of the K-Bar-C ranch, where there would be many other homesteaders someday. "How's it going?"

Cody tipped his junior-size Stetson back with a forefinger, mimicking the cowboys he'd seen in town. "Way cool. Rebel is the best ever!"

"Yes, he is." The gentle gelding plodded along, his head low and swinging with every step. So far, he'd ignored grouse flying up in front of his nose, a pair of deer bounding through the trees and had sidestepped an armadillo trundling across the path. For an inexperienced nine-year-old rider, Rebel was worth his weight in gold.

She dismounted and wrestled with the rusted hook and chain, opened the gate and led her horse through, then waited for Cody to pass. "We'll just leave this open while we ride. Miranda tells me that the Home Free program owns over five hundred acres of open pasture adjoining our land, and she says it's okay to ride back here for now."

Cody lifted a water bottle from his horn bag—the small saddlebags hanging from either side of his saddle horn—and took a long swallow. "We shoulda brought a picnic supper."

"Maybe next time. I'm sure we'll be riding here a lot."

The plat maps she'd studied showed that the western edge of her property curved to the west a mile or so from her pasture gate. There, if she'd guessed right, they'd almost be within sight of the main barns and house at the Four Aces.

With luck, they might see someone across the fence and strike up a casual conversation. A ranch hand who'd worked with her father would be perfect, because Clint had made it clear enough that she wasn't welcome on his ranch, or near his precious son.

"This is just like in the movies," Cody breathed. "I bet there were cowboys and Indians here once."

"There still are," she said dryly.

Cody rolled his eyes. "You know what I mean, like the Old West. Can we gallop?"

"Western horses *lope*. But no, I think we need to work more on jogging first. I'll jog, and you see if you can make Rebel jog, too. Just squeeze with your lower legs and click your tongue at him if he doesn't go."

Boots moved into a nice slow jog with the barest pressure of her calves. Looking over her shoulder, she saw Rebel still plodding along half asleep. "Well, try nudging him with both heels, then…okay, now try again, harder."

Rebel belatedly lifted his head and must've realized he was being left behind. He sped up into a rough, fast trot, with Cody hanging on to the horn and laughing as he bounced haphazardly in the saddle. Once they caught up, the old gelding slowed to match Boots's speed.

"I did good, right? I stayed on, and I made him go!"

It had likely been herd instinct rather than boy power that launched the horse briefly into second gear, but Kristin just gave Cody an encouraging smile. "You're getting better every day."

They followed the fence line, winding through stands of cedar and live oak, over sandy, pebbled ground and several grassy, low-lying meadows. Rocky crags jutted out of the hillsides, and at the top of each rise, the beauty of the rolling land made her wish she were good with watercolors.

Her hope of seeing someone from the neighboring ranch faded when they reached a tumbledown line shack in a hollow several miles from home. A glance at her watch told her it was time to head back.

"Cool! Can we explore it?" Cody leaned out of his saddle to peer at the broken timbers and sagging walls.

"No." Visions of rattlesnakes and scorpions hiding there made her speak too sharply. "Stay on your horse, Cody!"

Startled, Cody twisted around to look at her. With a cry he lost his balance and slid into a heap on the ground at his horse's feet. "Ouch!" he yelped, jerked his hand back. "Stickers!"

Rebel promptly lowered his head and nibbled at dry tufts of grass, apparently unfazed by the fall, and grateful for any opportunity to graze.

Dismounting, Kristin tied Boots to a nearby cedar tree, then eased over to grab Rebel's reins. She hunkered down next to Cody. "Are you okay, honey?"

"No! Look." His lower lip trembling, he held up a hand festooned with a haze of fine, nearly invisible cactus spines. "They burn—really bad." He lifted his tear-filled gaze up to his saddle. "How am I gonna get back up there?"

"No worries, sweetie. I'll lift you up, so you don't need to pull yourself up with that hand. I'm sure Rebel will just follow Boots home so you won't have to guide him at all."

"But it *hurts*."

It certainly wasn't going to be a fun trip home for him, even with his horse on autopilot. By the time they reached home each little cactus spine would have inflamed the skin around it, making the removal with tweezers even more painful.

"I know it hurts, sweetie. Here let me help you stand up." Hooking the joint of her elbow under his other arm, she hoisted him to his feet. "Now, let me—"

At a movement along the cedar-crested ridge to the west she fell silent, her pulse tripping. There shouldn't be any large predators out here— nothing more than coyotes—but she'd glimpsed something larger. A horse?

"What's wrong, Mom? What do you see?" His voice tinged with panic, Cody grabbed her arm with his good hand.

A second later she breathed a sigh of relief as a horse and rider emerged from the trees far beyond the Four Aces fence line. "Just someone else out riding."

He looked up at her with damp eyes. "Maybe he has tweezers."

The broad-shouldered rider started down the long hill toward them. "I sort of doubt it, Cody."

"But you'll ask, right? Please?"

They were probably close to the Four Aces buildings, but a lone woman and child could still be at risk in an isolated place. The guy heading their way could be anyone.

"I'll ask. But first let's get you up on your horse."

He gingerly grabbed for the horn with his good hand as she gave him a leg up into the saddle, then she remounted Boots. By the time she'd reached over to knot the ends of Rebel's reins for Cody, so they couldn't fall to the ground, the other rider had loped to the fence line.

At first glance she thought he was Ryan, with those blue eyes and wavy black hair, but where Ryan was toned and muscular, this man was thickset and developing a heavy belly that hung over the trophy buckle on his belt. Trevor, she figured, though she'd only met him briefly many years before.

"Howdy, ma'am. Everthin' goin' all right? Did the boy get hurt?"

"That's Hayden's dad," Cody stage-whispered. "I see him at football practice all the time."

"Just a little tumble into some cactus...and an unhappy boy," she called to him. "No broken bones, but thanks for asking."

"Trevor Gallagher." He touched the brim of his hat. "And you must be Miz Cantrell. I've seen you and the boy at school."

"Just Kristin is fine. This is my son, Cody. We just moved into the place next door."

He smiled at them. "Come on over here and let me take a look."

Kristin and Cody rode alongside the fence, and Cody held out his hand.

"Whoo-eee, I bet that stings." Trevor gave him a man-to-man appraisal. "You're one tough cowboy, let me tell you." He paused, considering, then reached for the cell phone clipped to his belt. "My wife, Donna, is good at taking those out, but our house is on the other side of the Four Aces. The main place is closer. She could meet us there, if you want to take care of this before you go home. She's a whiz with tweezers...though I'm sure your mom is, too."

Kristin bit her lower lip. "But our horses—how far is it?"

He pointed to the south. "There's a gate down in that next draw—we can get you through there. If we need to, we can trailer your horses home. It'll be dark before you know it."

Remembering Clint's harsh last words at the clinic, she hesitated. Alone, she wouldn't care, but there was no way she wanted to risk Cody witnessing his wrath. He'd seen entirely too much of that from his own father. "Are you sure this will be okay…with Mr. Gallagher?"

Trevor shrugged. "Why not? He's holed up in his office anyway. He almost never comes out to the barn."

She would've done anything to take back her sharp words that made Cody lose his balance. She'd gladly have taken the cactus spines in her own hand. But there *was* a silver lining. While they were at the Four Aces, she could ask a few questions.

She owed her dad that much.

THE THREE OF THEM tied their horses to the hitching rail in front of a long, low horse barn, and Trevor escorted them inside to an office, where Cody could rinse his hands in the adjoining bathroom.

Trevor's wife walked in minutes later, her long black ponytail brushing the waistband of her jeans.

She was, without a doubt, one of the loveliest women Kristin had ever seen—even in jeans and a plain cotton shirt. Her oval face and dark, expressive eyes probably turned heads wherever she went.

She offered her hand to Kristin. After a round of introductions, Donna smiled at Cody. "I hear you had an adventure."

He looked at her in awe and held out his hand, palm up.

Donna withdrew a plastic bag from her back pocket and offered it to Kristin. "I've got a couple of these tweezers. Maybe we can both work on him...if that's okay?"

"Thanks." Kristin took out one of the tweezers. "I really appreciate this."

Donna directed Cody to the chair behind the desk and switched on a bright halogen desk light, then pulled up chairs for Kristin and herself on either side of him.

He winced as they removed the first few spines, then sat still and quiet. When Kristin heard a rustle of movement at the door and looked over her shoulder, she knew why he was suddenly being so stoic. Two dark-haired children were hovering at the door, whispering to each other.

"Okay, you two," Donna said without looking up. "Come on in and be polite. Introduce yourselves to our new neighbors, you hear?"

"Yes, ma'am." The boy sidled farther into the room with his taller sister at his heels and shot a brief, shy glance at Kristin. "I'm Hayden, and this is my sister, Sara."

"Hayden is in fourth grade with Cody. Sara is a year older," Donna said as she deftly removed another cactus spine. "You two do your chores yet?"

"Yes, ma'am," Sara said shyly. With her long black hair and dark eyes, she was definitely on her way to being as beautiful as her mother. "The black momma cat had her kittens. We found them up in the hay."

"Maybe when we're done here, you could take Cody up to see them." Donna raised an eyebrow at Cody. "If you'd like to, that is."

He swallowed hard and nodded.

After another ten minutes, Donna brought the lamp closer and ran a practiced forefinger over Cody's palm with a feather-light touch. "I think we got it. Kristin, take a good look." Her mouth tipped into a wry grin. "I guess I plumb took over, but you're the professional."

Kristin laughed. "Not with cactus emergencies."

She'd seen Donna and Trevor exchange quick glances when she'd mentioned her last name, then Trevor had given a subtle shake of his head. From that point Kristin had felt guarded, wondering what that gesture meant, yet hesitating to ask while Cody could overhear.

Donna reached for a bottle of soothing lotion and smoothed it over his hand. "Good job, Cody. I haven't ever seen anyone sit so still for something like this. You want to go see those cats?"

He looked to Kristin for approval, then slipped out of his chair.

"Not too long, honey. We've got quite a ride home, and not much daylight."

Donna waved away her concern. "Trevor already brought up the horse trailer. He'll give y'all a ride home."

The kids raced out of the office, leaving Kristin and Donna to rearrange the chairs and set the desk back in order.

"I can't thank you enough. You and your husband were both so kind to help us out."

"It's nothing, really. I had to bring the kids over to do their chores, anyway, and Trevor doesn't mind a little trip like that." Donna walked over to a table in the corner and lifted a glass carafe of coffee. "I don't know how long this has been here, but I could make us a fresh pot." When Kristin started to demur, she added, "I don't imagine they'll be back directly. Kittens are quite a draw, and I suppose my kids will want to show Cody their horses and 4-H calves."

Donna busied herself rinsing out the pot and starting a fresh one in the tiny kitchen area of the large office. Searching through the cupboards, she found a new package of Oreo cookies, which she opened and shook out onto a plate. Then she retrieved cups and packets of sweetener and creamer.

"It's nice to meet our new neighbors," Donna

said as she set a tray of coffee and cookies on a small coffee table. "Have a seat."

Kristin took one of the high-backed leather chairs facing a dark plate glass window. A blur of motion swept past, and belatedly she realized she was facing an indoor arena. "Someone's riding out there?"

Donna leaned close to the glass. "I'm not sure who. Garrett's back—Trevor's younger brother— or it could be Ryan. It's light enough out there during the day, but I think I'd better give him some light." She moved to an electrical panel on the wall by the door, and instantly the arena was bathed in bright fluorescent light.

At the far side, Ryan loped a gleaming black colt in smaller and smaller circles, then he reined him into an effortless inside rollback to come out loping on the opposite lead.

Donna watched him for a moment before lifting a coffee cup and some cookies from the tray and sinking into the chair next to Kristin's. "He's good, isn't he?"

"More than."

"I think it helps him a lot, coming outside to work the horses. Therapy, of sorts." She studied Kristin over the rim of her cup, then lowered it and held it with both hands on her lap. "I understand you two have some history."

"A little." Kristin watched the horse and rider,

rather than meet the other woman's eyes. "I moved away when I was a child, but met him in college. We dated, broke up. The usual." From the corner of her eye, she saw the troubled look on Donna's face. "I'm sure I was just one of many."

"I'd probably just started dating Trevor back then." Donna worried at her lower lip with her perfect, white teeth. "I'm sorry you and I didn't meet back then."

"I was only here at the ranch once." A visit intended to be a joyous meet-my-family celebration…but one that had ended up being the most awful day of her life. Kristin forced a smile. "It's ironic, being here again after all these years. I had no idea that my land was next to this ranch… at least, not till I started moving in and missed my road a few times. The name of your ranch is listed on the No Trespassing signs all along the highway."

"Most land around here is leased to hunters, so we try to keep out the poachers." Donna watched Ryan dismount, toss a stirrup over the saddle and loosen the girth, then lead the horse out of the arena. "It's a nice coincidence that Ryan happens to be in town, now. I hear you two ran into each other."

"Briefly."

Donna's eyes twinkled. "And?"

"It was on a professional basis. *Only.*"

"There's no chance…?"

"None." Clint had been vicious on that cold, long ago day when he threatened to ruin her family if she didn't break up with Ryan. She'd had no doubt he would follow through.

He'd also told her he would force Ryan to leave school and go back to the ranch.

Devastated, she'd complied. When Ryan tried to dissuade her, she'd blurted out the first lie she could think of—that she never wanted to be a rancher's wife. That she wanted country clubs and money, not dust and cattle.

He'd believed her and he'd walked away.

Heartbroken, she pined for months, wishing he'd come after her. But he hadn't called or written. He hadn't missed her at all.

The irony was that she'd actually ended up, on the rebound, with a guy who'd had the country club and money. A guy who'd been a terrible mistake.

She glanced at her watch. Time was flying. Through the window facing the drive, she could see dusk had fallen.

"I do have a question." The sound of children chattering was close, but Kristin plowed ahead. "I understand my father worked here a couple years ago."

Donna dropped her gaze. "Yes, he did."

"Did you work with him? Talk to him much?"

"No...not really...and he was here less than a year." Donna swirled the remaining coffee in her cup. "The kids were seven and eight then. I was either home with them or commuting to my old job, which was two hours travel each day."

Kristin took a steadying breath. "I heard he was fired."

Donna didn't answer for so long that Kristin finally touched her arm. "Please, tell me."

The younger woman glanced over her shoulder and lowered her voice. "Clint is a hard man, bless his heart. He comes roaring in from Austin unexpectedly, doesn't like something, and heads roll. He's fired a lot of people over the years. *Good* people."

"My dad...was there a fight? A big argument?"

"I—I wouldn't know about that. Things are—" She stopped abruptly and seemed to withdraw into herself. "Your father is gone. There's no use worrying about the past, is there? Just let it be."

The kids burst into the room. "The truck is running, and Dad has the horses loaded," Sara exclaimed. "And we told Cody he could have a kitten, but not till they're older. He wants the one with black spots."

Standing, Donna tousled her son's hair, clearly relieved by the distraction. "I think you children should be asking Cody's mom before you start giving him any cats."

All eyes swiveled to Kristin.

"Please, Mom. It's gonna be really cool. It's got one black ear and one white, and it has a bull's-eye on one side."

"Sounds like quite a looker," she said dryly. "Let's see how you do with your horse chores during the next six weeks, first."

Cody's face fell. "Awww, Mom. They could give it to someone else!"

"I promise we won't," Donna assured him. "If you do what your mom says, we'll talk about it again when the kittens are old enough."

Trevor walked into the room, took off his hat and smiled apologetically at Kristin. "The truck is ready to roll, but I forgot about my Loveless County Cattleman's meeting tonight." He ducked his head in obvious embarrassment. "I'd skip it, but I'm...uh...the president this year."

"Oh, please...don't think twice. There's still enough moonlight so we can ride." Kristin offered her hand. "I'm just grateful for your help with Cody."

A taller figure stepped inside the tack room, and though he was behind Trevor and Donna, she didn't have to see him to know who it was.

"I'll drive," he said.

The deep voice resonated right through her, and her mouth went dry. Cody let out a whoop and raced out the door, but she felt no such surge of joy.

Another awkward meeting…a drive of a few miles that would seem like eternity.

This was her lucky day.

CHAPTER EIGHT

THE DRIVE HOME in Ryan's truck was as awkward as she'd expected. She couldn't think of a blessed thing to say.

Cody couldn't stop talking.

He peppered the man with questions about horses and armadillos and being a soldier who could shoot people.

She looked across the cab and saw Ryan's skin blanch, a muscle ticking at the side of his jaw. But to his credit he gave nonchalant, vague answers and then steered the questions back to safer ground.

She could see a big case of hero worship building, from the way Cody hung on his every word.

Bad news, because there was no way Ryan would be a permanent part of Cody's future, and this would lead to one more disappointment in her son's young life.

While most of his friends' grandparents were still in their lives, he'd barely known his Grandpa Nate, and the death of his dear Grammy Cantrell two years ago had broken his heart. The disinterest of his father and grandparents on *that* side of the family tree had hurt and confused him.

Night had fallen by the time they'd driven down to her barn and unloaded the horses. Crickets chirped and a far-off family of coyotes cried to the moon, the immature voices of the younger ones adding a discordant note to the haunting chorus.

"I think they need singing lessons," she teased as she unbuckled Rebel's halter and sent him out into the pasture with Boots.

Even in the moonlight, she could see Cody roll his eyes. *"Mo-om."*

"But they're better than me when I sing in the shower." She gave him a playful nudge with her elbow. "Go toss the horses some hay, will you? There's a bale right inside the barn."

Ryan was watching her, his eyes intent, almost curious, as if he couldn't quite place who she was anymore. She supposed he couldn't—she wasn't that young, impressionable nineteen-year-old now. Life had changed her in so many ways in the intervening years, just as it had changed him into a dark and haunted stranger.

"A penny for your thoughts," he said, his voice somber.

"This is just so strange," she said after a moment of thought. "I know you, yet I don't at all. And I could never even begin to understand what you've been through. We were such babies back in college weren't we? We believed that anything was possible."

"Innocence can be lost in many ways," he said cryptically. He closed the tailgate of the horse trailer and started for the truck. "Make sure you get to the football game tomorrow. It will mean a lot to Cody."

"Of course. I already planned to be there."

"And you should try to get Cody's dad here. That kid is hurting."

His words still stung as she watched him drive away. Even from that first day when he brought Cody home, he'd implied that she wasn't a careful mom. His opinion of her obviously hadn't changed, but she *had* planned to be there for Cody tomorrow. With or without that curt reminder.

And he had no idea just how traumatic it could be if Ted actually did show up.

ON THEIR THIRD MORNING at the Homestead Clinic, Kristin and Max had two well-baby physicals, an old-timer with arthritis and three people who simply wanted to check out the clinic "for future reference."

Max drummed his fingers on the counter in the lab, where he had reorganized the supplies four times since Tuesday morning. "I know I'll look back someday and regret saying this, but I really want this place to be busy."

"It will be. Just give it time. We have two patients this afternoon, and the *Homestead Herald* always comes out on Friday. Our notice will be good news to the people who haven't seen our sign because they don't get into town much. People are going to love having a local clinic again."

Max's eyebrows lifted. "*Love* is a tad strong, don't you think? Our first patient certainly hasn't been back."

"And he hasn't answered my phone messages, either. Before the HIPAA privacy laws took effect we could've called Clint's family, laid out the bad news, and his son would have him back in a hurry. Now, unless he signs a release, we can't say a word to anyone but him."

"So…what can we do now? Checkers? Scrabble? I think we've cleaned and polished and organized this place to the nth degree."

He was just in his early forties, but Max seemed more like the kind of grandfather she'd longed for as a child, rather than someone just ten years older. She grinned back at him. "Actually, I have an appointment with the sheriff over our lunch hour."

"You do have a dark and dangerous past." He feigned horror. "I *knew* it."

Laughing, she dropped her cell into her bag. "I think you're safe here. In fact, knowing that I work with a nurse who bench-presses three hundred pounds makes me feel safe, too."

She strolled across Main Street and cut across the lush green lawn of the courthouse. Following the signs, she skirted the massive stone building and went around to a back entry. The receptionist smiled and waved her toward a chair in the small waiting room outside several closed office doors.

A few moments later, a tall, well-built man in his mid-thirties came out. His khaki Dockers, white shirt and tooled leather belt were hardly like the uniforms of the police back in Dallas, but he emanated an air of quiet authority that no one could miss. "Miss Cantrell? I'm Wade Montgomery."

She rose and shook his hand. "Thanks for seeing me today. I was afraid you might be off on some emergency, or something."

He grinned. "Nothing earthshaking so far today, but that changes by the minute. Come on back."

She liked him at once. His manner was easygoing right down to the Stetson hanging on the rack by the door. He waited until she sat, then dropped into the swivel chair behind his desk.

"How long have you been here in town?" she asked.

"I grew up here, but moved away for college and didn't come back until I became sheriff four years ago." He studied her over steepled fingers. "I have the advantage, I guess, since I'm on the Home Free committee. I know you're new in town, and have the place Jim Baxter used to lease—western edge of the K-Bar-C property, a half mile off the highway. And, I believe, you still have family here."

"You have a good memory."

He lifted a notebook at the side of his desk. "I cheated and looked you up."

"I think I need a notebook like that. I lived here until I was ten, and there are so many people here that I don't remember, or who seem vaguely familiar." It left her with a strange sense of disconnectedness.

"Don't let it bother you. I was away for a long time, too, and this town *has* changed a great deal."

He was one of the few people who'd been open and friendly to her since she'd come to town. She wished she didn't need to bring up her family's troubled past. "I…guess you were in town eighteen months ago, then. My father…"

His affable expression faded to one of regret. "My deputies and I were clear across the county at a six-vehicle pile up on the interstate. By the time I arrived at the scene of your father's accident, the ambulance had taken him to the hospital."

"My father drove that road all his life. The weather was good, and that particular curve isn't even sharp." She felt her lower lip start to tremble and swallowed hard. "I just can't understand how he could have veered off right there, in broad daylight."

"Unfortunately, we see single-car accidents all the time. Someone is distracted, or dozes off for an instant. Maybe a deer bounds across the road and they swerve. Sometimes it's alcohol, though your dad was fine. One guy I know was startled by a low-flying wild turkey that cracked his windshield. He ended up in the river."

"I don't believe—" she hesitated, already seeing the doubt and resigned expectation in his eyes "—that my father's death was an accident. Maybe someone forced my father off the road, or damaged his truck beforehand."

"I understand. Believe me, we all want to second-guess these things a hundred different ways. We want a reason. Something—or someone to blame."

"But how do you know for *sure?*"

"Once the wrecker got his truck up on the road, we checked it over. There was a lot of rollover damage, but the steering wheel and brakes seemed fine."

"But you said the truck was damaged. There could've been paint marks from another vehicle, say, ramming into the side of it at that curve?

Marks you might've missed?" She saw the sympathy in his eyes. "I'd like to see the report."

"There was an investigation, ma'am. There was no evidence of skid marks from another vehicle. No witnesses. Interviews of people who knew him well uncovered no enemies." Wade swiveled his chair, stood and went to a bank of files along the wall. After thumbing through a number of tabbed folders he withdrew one and brought it back to the desk. "I'm not sure if you want to see these. They aren't of your father at the scene, but the damage to his truck is pretty significant. And…I believe there was some blood."

"Please." She gingerly opened the file to find a slim stack of documents. Behind them was an envelope of photos. Time slowed to a crawl. She dreaded the evidence of her father's death, yet needed, finally, to put her doubts to rest.

She dealt the four-by-six color photos out onto the desk, one by one. The crumpled front end of his '67 Chevy. The twisted bed and tailgate, showing the crushing damage to the roof of the cab—as if a giant had slammed his foot on it. The sides of the vehicle, battered and muddy. Clumps of grass hanging from the jagged spikes where the side view mirrors had been torn away. A narrow streak of bright crimson trailing down the side of the driver's side door.

Sadness and nausea welled until they almost

clogged her throat. "I—I didn't realize," she whispered as she sat back in her chair and rested her fingertips against her eyelids, concentrating on taking slow, even breaths.

She knew the truck well, because he'd driven it for decades. It had been a dented rust bucket from bumper to bumper even before the accident, a junker pieced together with different colors on each fender and a door painted primer-gray. Rust had already turned the quarter panels to fragile lace.

It was a truck that spoke of little success and even less hope for the future. Given its condition and preexisting dents, plus the mud and the grass and the damage from the accident itself, finding any sort of evidence would have been a sheer stroke of luck.

She felt a gentle touch at her shoulder and opened her eyes to find the sheriff offering her a glass of cold water. She accepted it and held it against her cheek, until her stomach quit rolling and she didn't feel quite so dizzy.

She managed a smile. "Thank you. I didn't mean to doubt your investigation, but I needed to know."

"I'm sorry about your loss, Ms. Cantrell. Death is hard, but death with no reason is even more difficult."

"That isn't quite what I meant." She slid the

photographs back into the envelope, closed the folder and handed it back to him. "I now know that evidence at the scene would've been very difficult to gather, but I'm still not convinced his death was accidental. If I wanted to find that old truck, where would I look?"

He studied her for a moment. "I know it's hard to let go of this, but—"

"I need to find it. Please."

He blew out a deep breath. "Out behind Buddy's Auto Shop. He keeps a lot of old vehicles for parts. But it's been eighteen months, ma'am. I expect that old truck has been crushed and melted down by now. There wasn't much left of it as it was."

"I hope I can find something, because there's not much left of my dad's honor, either."

COACHING FOURTH GRADE football had to be about as frustrating as trying to herd cats, but the little fellers were so serious, so determined, that Ryan could only lean against the hood of his truck and grin.

Few of them could hang on to the ball if it inadvertently landed in their hands. Some of them ran the wrong way, or bent over to study things they found in the grass. The ones who did run the right way tended to trip and fall if they got up too much speed. Cody had missed a half-dozen catches.

The parents rimming the makeshift football field set up in the school yard were something to watch, too, but he didn't like them nearly as much. Several fathers were yelling at their sons, impatient and angry, as if the world depended on the next haphazard play. Some of the moms were getting into it a little too much, as well.

If he was a dad, he'd be *cheering* his son on....

But that was as unlikely as a Central Texas ice storm in July.

He'd dated women along the way and had enjoyed treating them well. But none of them had even come close to making him feel like settling down. None of them since Kristin—and what a big mistake *that* had been.

A single male voice, rife with irritation, rose above the others. Ryan shifted his weight against the pickup and scanned the crowd, wishing the jerk would just shut up or leave. What did that do to a kid, hearing his dad berate him in front of everyone else? What kid would even want to try?

He surveyed the crowd again and then picked the man out of the crowd. He was a tall, slender guy standing off by himself, dressed in some sort of corporate getup. The whole nine yards—a well-cut jacket, crisply pressed pants, perfect hair with every strand in place.

From the back, Ryan could see that his ears were red with anger and as he turned....

Teddy Peters. He hadn't changed that much since college. He still had the pale complexion, splotched now with red patches on his cheeks, the thin, disapproving mouth.

Ryan turned away in disgust, wondering again how Kristin could've ever married someone like Teddy. Of course, she'd given money her highest priority. But how could that have outweighed everything else about someone who'd been such a supercilious fraternity twit in college?

He and Ryan had never been friends. Seeing the guy in action on campus had been more than enough basis to avoid him.

Ryan jerked his truck keys out of his pocket, but something made him turn back and search the playing field.

Hayden was still out there, of course, bursting with energy and having the time of his life.

But Cody... Frowning, Ryan scanned the field again. Even with the same oversize uniforms on, he'd picked out the boy right away, and now...

At the far end of the field he finally saw a woman kneeling next to a boy, who stood with his head bowed and his hands hanging loose at his side.

He knew in an instant that Kristin was trying to repair the damage...and that this was probably his fault. He'd pushed her to get the poor kid's father here today.

He ignored the increasing pain in his knee as he strode across the grass to the far side of the parents cheering on their kids, and drew to a stop within inches of Ted. The man was oblivious, still glaring at his son instead of trying to console or praise him.

"Ted," Ryan growled. He lowered his voice another notch. "I see you've come out here to make your son's day."

Startled, Ted jerked away. "Who—" Recognition dawned in his face as he surveyed Ryan from head to toe, and his smug expression turned to contempt. "Well, look who's here."

"The question is, why you're here, if all you want to do is belittle your son."

"The kid doesn't even try." Ted sneered, clearly irritated. "But that's hardly your concern, is it?"

Ryan eased farther into the man's space, crowding him back a step. "It's the concern of every decent adult here. How do you think you make Cody feel? Special? Loved? Or maybe the issue is how it makes *you* feel. Give you a sense of power, maybe? Maybe make you feel like a big man?"

"Look, Gallagher, back off. I hardly think threatening me in front of all these people is wise. Lay a hand on me, and I have a hundred witnesses."

Ryan sensed someone come up behind him,

and glanced over his shoulder. An older woman and her husband stood glaring at Ted.

"Frankly, I think you're pathetic," the woman said, her voice hard. "I've listened to you for the past fifteen minutes, and I think you should be reported to the county hotline for the way you treat that boy." Her husband touched her arm, but she shook him off. "I don't care, Frank. Verbal abuse is every bit as painful as being hit."

"I'm not sure all the 'witnesses' are on your side, *Teddy*." Ryan nodded toward Cody and Kristin. "You're going over there to apologize to Cody. You're going to explain that you didn't mean it, and you're going to tell him that he's a super kid. Make him *believe* it...or I'll report you myself."

Ted stared back at Ryan, then his eyes veered toward the older couple and another woman who'd come to join them. He lifted his chin. "I would've talked to him anyway. Stay out of my business."

His anger simmering, Ryan held Ted's gaze until the other man finally broke eye contact and took a faltering step back. "Now, Ted. Undo the damage you did to that poor kid."

"It was ridiculous of Kristin to insist I come for this little recess activity, anyway. I left clients. An important meeting. And for what?" Ted stalked toward his son, his back rigid. He lingered for just a few minutes, dropped an awkward pat on Cody's shoulder, then he got into a gleaming black BMW and drove off.

It wasn't enough. Ryan could see that in the boy's slumped shoulders and the way Kristin was glaring at Ted's car as he disappeared down the street.

Kristin had made bad choices. Well, everyone had made some bad ones all those years ago, but it was clear she'd paid dearly.

Squaring his shoulders, Ryan sauntered over to join her, and hoped he could help make things right for her little boy.

CHAPTER NINE

RYAN STAYED a few yards back, unsure whether or not he should interfere with Kristin's pep talk.

"Cody, you know your dad gets impatient about things." Sitting back on her heels, Kristin gave him a conspiratorial smile. "He was never good at sports and he really doesn't understand them. Believe me, you're doing a fine job out on that field, and I'm proud of you."

Cody pulled off his team shirt and dropped it on the ground. "I'm slow and stupid, and I didn't even catch the ball. Not once."

"You're just as good as every other boy out there. Fourth graders aren't *supposed* to be perfect, and none of those other kids are, either. They're just learning the basics and practicing so they can get better."

Cody's attention veered to the playing field, where Hayden caught the football on the run and ran the length of the field. The despair in Cody's eyes spurred Ryan forward and he rested a hand on Kristin's shoulder. "How much are you doing with him at home?"

She pulled away and gave Ryan a cold glare as she stood up. "He's just been to two practices so far. We'll start playing catch with the football, I suppose. And…whatever the coach tells us to do."

"Not enough." Ryan eyed Cody thoughtfully. "Some of these town kids get to play all the time. All those neighborhood pickup games with their friends give them an advantage."

Cody shuffled his feet in the grass and studied his shoelaces, but he was clearly listening to every word.

"What do you say to throwing the ball with Hayden and me after school? Maybe a couple times a week? You could come home on the school bus with him. He needs the extra work, too."

Cody's head bobbed up in disbelief. "*Hayden* does?"

"Well, he's got the same problem you do— no neighbor guys around. If it's okay with your mom, you two could practice together. Throwing and catching are important skills in this game." Ryan cocked his head, taking the boy's measure. "You're both strong kids with a lot of talent. What do you say?"

Cody jammed his hand in his jeans pockets, trying to look nonchalant, but the hope in his eyes gave him away as he turned to his mom. "Can I?"

"I don't know." She bit her lower lip. "I'm sure the Gallaghers are busy people, Cody."

"Let me clear it with Hayden's mom and dad, and then we'll get back to you. I'll bet we can work something out a couple times a week." Ryan glanced over at the coach, who was lining up the two "teams" for another play. "Right now, though, you'd better get over there, so those guys don't get to learn more than you."

Cody flashed a grateful grin at Ryan, jerked on his shirt and sped across the field. His mother shielded her eyes against the late-afternoon sun, her shoulders sagging.

"I try. Honestly, I try," she murmured. She smiled wearily at Ryan. "I appreciate what you said to Cody. I just hope it works out to play with Hayden—he'll be so crushed if this falls through."

"I can't imagine why we can't get them together one way or another. If Donna has other commitments for Hayden right after school, then you could bring Cody over later. I can certainly make time to work with the boys."

A faint blush colored her cheeks. "I imagine everyone here heard Ted being his charming self again."

He wanted to ask how she could have married the guy. What it had been like all this time, for her and Cody. But he'd lost the right to ask such personal questions long ago. Instead, he lifted a shoulder in a noncommittal shrug. "I feel sort of responsible. I told you to invite him."

"He knew about it, and I'd already planned to remind him, because he *should* come more often. Maybe he would learn more about his son, and loosen up a little. It hurts Cody terribly that he has so little interaction with his dad."

"Kids grow up fast, and you sure can't go back later." Though Clint had *never* had the inclination to spend father-son time with his three boys. "That's a mistake a man should never make."

Kristin seemed to read Ryan's mind, because her expression grew sympathetic. "You'd be a good father, Ryan." She glanced across the field, to where Trevor was exchanging high-fives with his son. "Trevor sure is."

Not like your father.

He knew what she was thinking. She'd met Clint only once, when Ryan brought her home to meet the family, and Clint hadn't been at the ranch long that weekend. Surly and impatient, wrapped up in some sort of political project, he'd been the antithesis of a congenial host…and nowhere close to anyone's image of a loving parent.

"That won't happen for me." The thought of fatherhood was too foreign to even contemplate. "I look forward to time with my niece and nephew while I'm still here, though."

"You haven't found some pretty little lieutenant in the service?" Kristin teased.

"I'm not looking." Uncomfortable, he tipped the brim of his Western hat and started to turn, but she reached out to stop him.

"Before you leave...I've left several phone messages for your dad, and he hasn't answered. Does he check his machine?"

"All the time." Concerned, Ryan searched her face. "What's wrong?"

"I just need to talk to him. He needs to come back to the clinic. Soon."

"Were his tests okay? The blood work and the EKG?

"I need to talk to him directly, and then he can decide what to share. I'm sorry, it's the law."

Ryan sighed. The first two visits had been a test of wills. Though Trevor had agreed to making the second trip, only Ryan had been able to coerce that old man into action, and even then they'd been a good fifteen minutes late.

"I'll do what I can to get him there, but no guarantees. He wasn't all that pleased the last time."

Watching her as she walked away reminded him of his college days at the University of Texas-Austin, and the hot, early-September afternoon he'd been sitting on a low stone wall outside Benedict Hall waiting for a buddy.

The prettiest girl he'd ever seen had walked by, her long blond hair cascading down her slender back, oversize sunglasses partially obscuring her delicate face. She'd stopped a few yards away to hunt through her unwieldy backpack for something, and when a breeze scattered some of her papers onto the grass, he'd considered it his lucky day.

He'd vaulted over the wall after them, and ended up talking to her for an hour. She was sweet and funny and smart. The fact that they'd both been born in the same small town had given them common ground. For the next six months they'd been inseparable, so sure their love would last forever that he'd proposed to her on Valentine's Day and taken her to meet his family the following weekend.

She'd walked out on him the next day, catapulting him from joy to misery in an instant.

How would their lives have been different if they'd stayed together? Would they have had children Cody's age? Would they have been happy? Or would they have ended up as just one more divorce statistic, like their parents?

Every time he saw her, he found himself increasingly drawn to her. But he'd been a fool once and it wouldn't happen again.

RYAN PUSHED AWAY from the desk and massaged his left shoulder, trying to work out the pain and stiffness. He glanced at the clock. Only *eleven* o'clock?

He'd awakened early and gone out to work Jazz, the young black gelding he'd been riding every day, then he'd helped Trevor with chores. That time had flown. The past two hours in the office had felt like ten.

After talking to Leland last Saturday, he'd started working on the books, sorting through overdue notes, misfiled papers and a bookkeeping system that seemed to have no system whatsoever. He was ready to pitch the antiquated computer out the window and shovel the contents of the file cabinets into a roaring bonfire.

If complete records had ever existed, they sure weren't in this office now. And if Clint walked in one more time and questioned his every move, he was going to pack his duffle bag and catch the next flight back to...

Ryan turned at the sound of shuffling footsteps at the door and found his youngest brother with one hand braced against the frame, his face sallow.

"Howdy, bro." Garrett's voice was filled with morning-after gravel, his words slurred. The undercurrent of resentment in his tone was loud and clear. "Ah, I see you're in here saving us all from ruin."

Ryan gave him a contemptuous once-over and raised his voice. "And I see you're awake."

Garrett flinched. "I'm drunk, not deaf." He moved into the room with the cautious balance of someone trying to avoid jarring a killer headache.

"That's hungover, not drunk, and you're a mess. Is this what you do all the time?" After arriving late Wednesday, Garrett had showered and headed into town. Apparently he'd stayed out most of the night and slept most of Thursday, then took off again last night.

"S'pose so." Garrett eased himself into one of the leather upholstered chairs in the office, propped a booted foot on the other one, and slouched until he was nearly prone. "Less I'm chasin' the bulls. Got no place to go this weekend."

A strip of Ace bandaging showed beneath the cuff of his white Western shirt. Curious, Ryan moved closer and brushed the hair back from Garrett's forehead. Sure enough, a deep yellow-green bruise covered the left side. "You get this in a bar fight, or from that last bull?"

Garrett batted his hand away. "Bull," he growled.

"Eight seconds?"

"Made it to seven. He was a real good draw, and I was scoring high…then he sucked into a reverse spin and came right out from under me. Left me in the dirt."

So he'd been out of the money, which probably accounted for his return to the ranch. Trevor had said Garrett traveled with rodeo buddies, and avoided coming home as long as any of them were earning enough to keep gas in the truck and the next entry fees paid.

"What about your arm?"

"'S nothin'."

"Fracture? Sprain? Or do you just wear that Ace for decoration?"

Garrett glanced at Ryan, then looked away. "Banged up a little, is all."

"Were you seen by a doctor? Did you have X-rays?"

"No time. Danny and Trace had to make it to Albuquerque by tonight. So we came back here, they got Danny's truck and took off."

The sullen tilt of his mouth was so reminiscent of him as a child that Ryan had to curb a laugh. "Left you behind, did they?"

"Don't matter."

Ryan had already come across three substantial checks made out to Garrett over the past four months. "You thought you'd stop by, pick up some money and take off again. Am I right?"

"What's it to you?"

"Let me get this straight. You and Trevor stand

in line to inherit this place. Trevor's working his butt off here, you breeze through when you need money. Sounds fair."

"It's none of your business." He propped an elbow on the arm of his chair and gingerly touched his fingertips to his temple. "You...have no idea what's fair."

Ryan laughed out loud. *Fair* would have been a father who'd been close, loving, supportive. A father who wouldn't have stalled every dream and threatened to disown him if he didn't buckle. *Fair* would've been a father who made that threat in the heat of anger, but didn't follow through.

Ryan knew all about the fairness in Clint Gallagher's cold heart, but he just smiled grimly. "Maybe you wheedled money out of the past managers here at the ranch, but while I'm here that won't happen."

Garrett shot to his feet—the dramatic effect spoiled when he stumbled over his own legs in the process and then swayed until he caught his balance. "You can't do that."

"Try me." Ryan waved a hand toward the training pens outside. "Get sober, get that arm checked out. Then you can start riding colts and helping with chores around here. Earn your money, and you'll get your check in a month. You're twenty-six, Garrett. It's time to grow up."

"It isn't your decision." His voice filled with

loathing, Garrett shouldered Ryan belligerently as he passed on his way to the door. "You can get lost."

Pain sliced through Ryan's shoulder at the rough contact, followed by a roll of nausea in his stomach. But worse than that was his guilt over the two young brothers he'd left behind when he went into the service.

"I've been there, kid," he said softly, watching Garrett stalk toward the house. "And there's all kinds of ways to get lost. I'm just sorry you haven't found your way back yet."

CODY FIDGETED in his seat as his mom turned off the highway. Huge stone pillars rose on either side of the lane, supporting a heavy log suspended high overhead with The Four Aces carved on it in fancy letters. There were big flowering bushes flanking the entrance, too, and the road ahead was lined with trees and a white pipe fence that seemed to go on forever.

Before, they'd entered the ranch through a back pasture gate, and had left after dark. Now, in the bright, Saturday-morning sunlight, it all looked so grand, so different from their own place, that he suddenly felt very small and a lot more nervous. "What if it's a mistake? Maybe this wasn't really the day."

Mom glanced over at him and smiled. "Hayden's mom called just last night, honey."

"But what if they, like, don't really want me to come over? Maybe it's just a big favor, or something, and I'll be in the way."

"Donna said you were more than welcome. She said Hayden's looking forward to this, and if it works out, we'll try to get you two together on a regular basis."

He laced his fingers over his stomach. "My stomach feels weird."

"Really." Mom frowned, but kept her eyes on the road. "For how long?"

"Uh…all morning. Since I got up."

She cocked an eyebrow. "So that was *before* the three bowls of cereal and the hour you spent working on your fort in the barn? I sure heard a lot of pounding out there."

"Yeah. Only now it's worse. Maybe I'll have to throw up, or something."

She gave him a pat on the leg. "Let's see how this goes. You might feel a lot better once we get there."

The road went up and down hills, past rocky crags and stands of live oaks, a big pond surrounded by pines, then finally the ranch house came into view. From this angle, it was a whole lot bigger and fancier than he'd realized. What was it like to have so much money that you practically owned the world?

He could see Hayden's dad leading a horse into the barn, and a couple of men over by a pen of cattle. Someone was riding a horse in the big outdoor arena. Everywhere he could see, there were neat, white pipe-fenced corrals and pastures filled with horses or cattle.

By the time they pulled to a stop in a parking lot in front of the barns, Hayden was standing there, tossing a football in the air.

Mom reached for her door handle, then hesitated. "I might just sit in here and read for a while," she said. "Go on now —he's waiting for you."

Suddenly feeling shy, Cody slunk down in his seat.

Ryan came out of a nearby barn and sauntered up to his mom's window. "Thanks for bringing your son over."

"It's so nice of you to invite him."

Ryan shrugged. "It'll be good for everyone. I just need to wrap up a few things in the office, and then I'll be ready. The boys can hang out for a while. Knowing Hayden, he's probably got a million things he'd like to show Cody."

"The kittens, Mom," Cody stage-whispered, hoping she hadn't forgotten.

Ryan leaned down to peer through the window

at Cody. "I'm sure we have plenty of those." To Mom he added, "Either Donna or I can bring Cody home."

"I don't want to be any bother. I don't mind waiting, really."

"Donna says she'd love to have you come over for coffee, in that case." Ryan pointed to the road that led past the barns. "They're just a couple miles farther."

Cody climbed out of the truck and wandered over to Hayden. "You wanna practice while we wait for your uncle?"

Nodding, Hayden stepped back twenty paces and lobbed the ball at Cody. He caught it in a bear hug at his chest, then scrambled to send it back again. Out of the corner of his eye Cody saw his mom's truck pull away and the ball accidentally went wild, arcing way over Hayden's head. "Sorry."

Hayden ran after it and sent it flying back harder than the last time, and it stung Cody's hand so much that he dropped it on contact. "Hey!"

They stared at each other for a long moment, then Hayden turned away in disgust. *Loser.*

They weren't good friends at school. They were in the same classroom, though they sat across the room from each other, and there'd been a thread of competition between them in gym and at recess since the first day they met.

Now, that whispered word bit deep as Cody watched Hayden disappear into the barn. He stood alone in the empty parking lot, then wandered down the dark, cool aisle of the barn, wondering where Hayden had gone. *The jerk.* Who wanted to be friends with someone like him, anyway—just 'cause he had a rich grandpa and lived on a fancy ranch?

At the end of the aisle he heard voices on the other side of a half-opened double door, so he kept going—then froze when he heard Hayden's angry voice.

"I'm 'sposed to be nice to him, but I wanted to go to the horse sale with Dad today!"

A deeper male voice murmured something Cody couldn't quite hear.

"I don't care," Hayden said stubbornly. "I coulda gone if Mom hadn't made me stay home. Cody's a creep, and anyway, I *heard* about what his grandpa did. Mom and Dad were fighting about Nate last night, and I heard."

Feeling as if an iron fist had grabbed his stomach, Cody held his breath and eased forward until he could see around the corner. A man with the same dark hair as Ryan was leaning against the bumper of a pickup, a beer can lowered at his side and a cigarette in his other hand.

The man made a wide gesture toward Hayden with the beer. "You shouldn't eavesdrop on your parents, kid."

"Well, Uncle Ryan had to come home because of it. I know you don't like that, 'cause I heard you and him argue, too," Hayden shot back.

"You are the nosiest nephew I have," the man growled with a hint of exasperation.

"The *only* one you have," Hayden retorted, as if it were an old joke between them. "Anyway, it isn't fair. I heard Dad say Nate was Cody's grandpa, and that it was all Nate's fault that a *lot* of money disappeared. He stole it when he worked here, then he died, and no one ever found it. How come no one ever told *me*? Is that why Dad won't buy me a new four-wheeler?"

Cody felt himself go cold, then hot.

Grandpa Nate?

He took a step farther back into the shadows, humiliated. Every time the Gallaghers looked at him, were they thinking about what his grandpa did? Maybe even watching to see if Cody was a thief, too?

He spun on his heel and dashed down the aisle, ignoring the squeal of the door behind him and the call of his name.

Outside, he squinted in the bright sunshine as he scanned for any sign of his mother's truck. Then he started running down the road toward the highway. It had to be miles and miles away, but there was no way he wanted to stay here now—not with humiliation burning in his stomach and the sound of Hayden's scornful voice still ringing in his ears. Had he told kids at school already?

At the top of the first hill he stopped to catch his breath. Glancing behind him, he could see Hayden and his uncle standing in front of the barn, looking around—probably calling his name—though it was too far away to hear them.

He shaded his eyes as he studied the rolling hills to the east, considering the possibility of cutting across country to find his way home. *Not likely.* Heaving a sigh, he started toward the highway.

Sooner or later Mom would come by.

He wouldn't tell her about the lies he'd heard. She'd be upset—and what could she do about it anyway, since Grandpa was dead?

He would think up a story about why he'd started for home, and then make sure he never talked to Hayden or came to the Four Aces again.

CHAPTER TEN

AT THE SIGHT of a forlorn figure trudging along the side of the road, Kristin breathed a sigh of pure relief. She dialed the Four Aces number on her cell phone and tapped her fingers on the steering wheel of her truck until an unfamiliar male voice answered.

"Garrett here."

"This is Kristin. Tell Ryan I found Cody walking home. I'll have a talk with him about not running off like this, I promise you."

"Uh…good. That's good." He ended the connection abruptly, leaving her to wonder at the odd note in his voice.

The Gallaghers were all probably thinking Cody was impulsive and undisciplined, but that didn't matter now. All that mattered was seeing her son ahead. If he'd tried to cut across the pastures… She shuddered, imagining rattlers and scorpions, and envisioning him lost through the heat of the day. *And it's my fault,* she said to herself as she pulled to a stop. *He didn't want to come over here, and I made him anyway.*

She rolled down the window on the passenger's side and leaned across the seat. "Hey, buddy— need a lift?"

He stopped walking, but he kept his eyes forward, his hands clenched tight at his sides. She could see dusty tracks down his cheeks where he'd been crying, and without a ball cap to shade his face, his nose was already turning pink.

Without a word, he climbed into the truck and fastened his seat belt.

"Kind of a warm day for a hike, isn't it?" She checked the odometer. "You walked a whole mile and a half, honey."

He made some sort of unintelligible sound in response.

"You know that the Gallaghers have been looking for you? They've been searching all of their barns and corrals in case you went hunting for those kittens. When Ryan called me a few minutes ago, he was worried about you." She considered how much she should say. "It was very nice of them to ask you to come over, and it was wrong of you to just take off like that."

He stared out the side window as if he didn't even hear her.

"If you don't think this is a problem, maybe we'll need to look at grounding you for a while." When he still didn't respond, she added, "And that would include riding and television. I'm sorry, but—"

The cell phone on the seat jingled, and she grabbed it on the second ring.

"Kristin? This is Ryan. Garrett tells me you found Cody."

"On his way home. Without a word to any of you. I'm really sorry."

There was a long silence on the other end of the line, and then Ryan cleared his throat. "I've been talking to Garrett. I need to talk to you privately. Can I stop by your place in a half hour or so?"

A lecture, perhaps, on her lack of parenting skills? A tactful discussion regarding the end of any further visits to the Four Aces? "Sure. Why not."

There'd been a time when her world had revolved around Ryan Gallagher, but what he thought about her didn't really matter. Not anymore.

The sooner they got this little discussion over, the better.

KRISTIN SENT CODY on up to his room until lunch, then settled in at her newspaper-covered dining-room table with her shoe box of acrylic paints.

She'd just opened up the midnight blue when she heard heavy footsteps on the porch steps and a familiar voice calling her name.

"Come on in," she said, selecting a brush from the assortment soaking in a Mason jar of water. She dried it against a paper towel and dipped it in the paint, then began touching up the shadows on the bluebonnets she'd painted around the edge of a weathered board.

Maybe Ryan had some things to say, but she didn't need to give him her full attention.

He walked through the living room to join her at the table. "Nice," he said, as he studied the sign. "I'd forgotten this place was called Cedar Grove Farm. I don't think there's been a sign up for years."

"There is one—but it's old and faded, and hidden by some scrub cedars." She touched up another flower, then held the brush aloft. "But I'm sure you didn't come over to check out my beginner artwork."

He frowned, a muscle in his jaw flexing. "It's about Cody…we need to talk."

Sighing inwardly, she dropped her brush into the water glass with the others, and capped her jar of paint. "And?"

"I thought it strange that Cody took off like he did, because I knew he'd been looking forward to some extra football practice." Ryan cleared his throat. "I feel much of this is my fault, really. If I hadn't had those phone calls to make before noon…"

This wasn't what she'd expected at all, and a sixth sense sent a chill across her skin. She glanced toward the stairs leading up to the bedrooms, where Cody might still be able to overhear, then nodded toward the kitchen. "Maybe we should go in there to talk."

She bustled over to the coffeemaker and started a pot brewing, while Ryan stood looking out the windows by the kitchen table, his thumbs hooked in his back pockets.

He'd changed so much.

Not just the limp when he walked, or the way he favored that damaged shoulder. Even when he was simply conversing, there was a weariness in his eyes that didn't fade. But now…he seemed to carry the weight of the world.

She spilled some store cookies onto a plate and set them on the table, retrieved two mugs from the cupboard and poured the coffee. "Please, have a seat."

He tipped his head in acknowledgment, but simply stood behind a chair with his hands resting on the back. "I had a long talk with Garrett, and I'm not exactly sure where to start."

"Sit. Eat a cookie." She managed a smile, even though her stomach was tied in knots. "You'll feel better."

"Trevor took off for a horse sale this morning. Donna had already made plans for Cody to come over, so she wouldn't let Hayden go. He was upset, but that doesn't excuse his behavior." Ryan snorted with disgust. "He walked off after Cody arrived. He found his Uncle Garrett and said things he shouldn't have—things that Cody must have overheard, because Garrett saw the boy run out of the barn."

"Kids can be cruel sometimes. Maybe the boys can just talk it over."

"It's not that simple." Ryan splayed his fingers on the back of the chair, then pulled it out and sat down to face her across the table. "Hayden told Garrett he'd overheard his mom and dad arguing about Cody's grandfather. Hayden would've been just seven when Nate worked at the ranch, so I'm sure he hadn't realized until now that Cody and Nate were related."

"Dad worked for Clint off and on, through the years. They had some business deals together, too, but I think all of them went south." She shook her head. "Even at his funeral, I heard whispers about my dad being 'in Clint's pocket,' but I'll never believe that he would do anything underhanded." She blushed as she realized what she'd just said to Clint's own son. "Er...sorry."

"Isn't anything I haven't heard before." Ryan shrugged. "Oscar, our foreman, took off, leaving the financial records in a mess. Leland tried to sort it out before your dad was hired. Nate stayed

on just a few months until he quit...or was fired."
Ryan cradled his cup in both hands and studied
the steaming liquid. "I'm not sure who said the
words first, but Adelfa says they had quite an
argument."

"So Hayden talked about Nate being fired?"
That could hurt, she knew. Though Cody and his
grandfather had never been close, it could still
feel like a personal attack to hear those words
about your own flesh and blood. "That's not so
bad, really."

Ryan's eyes met hers. "After your father left this
ranch, Leland brought in a forensic accountant to
try to figure out the books. Records were missing
or altered, but the guy figured your father embezzled at least sixty grand in four short months.
Cody overheard that."

Kristin's heart faltered. "That's...that's impossible. My father was an honest man, and he had
nothing. Almost *nothing* in his bank accounts
when he died, and he drove a beat-up old truck.
Even if he thought about it, he'd have known
that Clint and Leland would keep a close eye on
things."

"Or...he might have figured that with the state
the financial records were in, it would be much
easier to filter more away. The losses might still
appear to be Oscar's errors coming to light."

Her anger flared. "So you think my father was

guilty. Where's your proof? Where are the police reports—the investigations?" She stood abruptly and braced herself against the table. "Why didn't I ever hear a thing about this? Or was it hushed up because your own father has a few things that ought not be revealed?"

Ryan lifted his hands in a placating motion. "Please—sit down, okay?"

She pushed away from the table and stalked across the room, then pivoted and came back to the table, her arms crossed. "Where is all that money, then? My father died just a few weeks after he left the Four Aces. He barely had enough money to cover his funeral."

"Clint hired a private investigator, as well as the forensic accountant." Ryan's tone was regretful. "The P.I. discovered a bank account in another small town, set up for an agricultural spraying business that doesn't exist. The deposits were always under ten grand...and cash withdrawals were made several thousand at a time. There may have been other accounts he hasn't been able to trace yet."

"You're wrong about my dad, and I'm going to prove it." Kristin glared at him, even though her heart was breaking. "Furthermore, I don't believe his death was an accident. With everything I've just heard, I'm even more sure. Now you tell me—who would want my father dead?"

RUNNING A HAND over his face to check for stubble, Clint scowled at his dim image in the mirror. It wasn't supposed to be this way. He'd worked hard all his life. He'd done right by his family. His constituents. He sat in his own pew at church every Sunday when he was in town.

He deserved better than bad eyes and a family that had fallen apart.

Right now Garrett was probably sleeping off another drunken night at the Saddle Up…unless he'd crashed at Trip Dooley's sleazy Rise and Shine Motel on the edge of town.

The thought of his young son drinking himself into oblivion made his stomach roil. The thought of him riding bulls was even worse.

Ryan had defied Clint almost from birth, had a way of staring Clint down as if he was dissecting every last flaw. Trevor was solid—a hard worker—but without imagination or brains.

But Garrett…

His favorite son. Garrett had inherited Clint's ambition and drive, his mother's charm. He'd chosen to throw away every golden opportunity rather than give up his obsession with rodeo, but one of these days he'd wake up and realize just how much time he was wasting. And then there'd be no stopping him. *If the right person was still there to guide him.*

Which was why Clint had finally agreed to his doctor's appointment today.

He dressed quickly, knotting his dark tie by feel rather than sight, assured of a good match by the fact that he wore only navy and black, and had long since ordered Adelfa to throw away any socks and ties that didn't coordinate.

The Homestead clinic nurse had been calling daily, leaving messages for him to come back about his lab work and EKG. He'd finally capitulated yesterday, agreeing to come in on Wednesday when the *real* doctor was there.

It was all a lot of waste, anyway, throwing money on doctoring something that was perfectly fine. His heart felt strong. Healthy. He wasn't a weakling like Enfield, who looked as if he had his hair styled and nails buffed—a man who was all hat and no cattle, far as Clint could see.

Pocketing his billfold, he slipped into his Italian loafers, ran his hands over his short cropped hair and went out to the kitchen where Adelfa would be waiting to hand him a cup of dark roast coffee on his way to Trevor's truck.

A familiar voice in the kitchen stopped him dead in his tracks before he walked in.

Clint Gallagher bowed to no one, but now he felt his pulse grow unsteady and he had to force himself to move forward.

Adelfa stood by the stove, her round face

wreathed in smiles. A tall, elegant figure stood facing her, one hand propped carelessly on the counter. Well-cut linen slacks molded to the woman's long, slender legs. A sweater—something in one of those nubbly, natural weaves—skimmed her graceful back.

"Ah, here he is," Adelfa beamed at him as if she'd just come across a great prize. "Look who is here—Señora Gallagher!"

As Lydia turned, he was struck—as always—by the loveliness of her sculpted cheekbones. The elegant flare of her eyebrows. The quiet beauty of her large, expressive eyes. She was—and always would be—the most beautiful thing in his life, despite the divorce.

She was also the one person in the world who could argue him to the ground with an amused and patient look in her eyes that made him angry enough to spit nails.

She gave him a leisurely head-to-toe assessment. "Nothing's changed here, I see. You're looking well."

"I wasn't expecting a visit."

"Ever the gracious host." Her musical laugh filled the room. "I believe you're supposed to say, 'And you're looking good, as well,' or some such pleasantry."

Adelfa, apparently sensing trouble, nodded to both of them and sidled out of the kitchen.

He knew his social graces—he hadn't risen to prominence in state politics by sounding like the backwoods kid he'd once been. But with Lydia, it was generally best to cut to the chase. "Why are you here?"

"Don't worry, dear. I want nothing from you. If you recall, I didn't even ask for much of anything in our divorce." She wandered over to the windows facing the sweep of lawn and beyond that, the stables. "I drove in from Dallas this morning because Ryan is here. I doubt I'll be much of a nuisance if I stay a few days."

A few days.

A few days of turmoil. Subtle insults traded over supper. Glances filled with hostility. Tension that had him popping antacids and Tylenol.

"That would be fine. Adelfa can prepare the guest room." He ground the words out. "I suppose now that Ryan is in Texas, it's convenient for you to see him?"

He caught a flash of hurt in her eyes, but then she lifted her chin and leveled a haughty stare at him. "I wasn't able to go to Walter Reed to see him, if that's what you mean. But I called him every day. Did you go? No, wait—you were too busy."

"Trevor and Garrett went." There'd been no point in going. He and Ryan had never gotten along, and the State Senate had been in session.

Still, Lydia's words cut deep. "But you can hardly judge, right? His own mother didn't bother."

"I...couldn't."

Something wasn't quite right, he realized. She'd always been angular, in a sophisticated Kate Hepburn way, but... "Why, Lydia?"

She lifted her hand in an airy wave. "You know, the usual. We had a showing at the gallery, and Harris was gone for a few weeks, so everything was up to me...and then there was a buying trip...."

At her longtime boyfriend's name, Clint bristled. He strode to the coffeemaker, poured himself a cup and lifted it in mocking salute. "I have an appointment. Make yourself at home."

LYDIA WRAPPED her arms around herself against a sudden chill as Clint walked out the door. It had always been like this. Fire and fuel, the two of them. They'd made so many mistakes. Selfish mistakes born of passion and stubbornness and personalities too strong to ever truly mesh. It had been the children who'd suffered the most.

But nothing of that painful past could be changed.

This would be her last chance to try to heal old wounds and make things right. And with any luck, she'd have enough time left to do it.

CHAPTER ELEVEN

KRISTIN GRINNED at the tall, lanky cowboy standing at the front desk of the clinic. With those green eyes and that thick brown hair, Ethan Ritter had to be quite a heartbreaker in these parts, though she also sensed a quiet reserve that probably kept most women at bay.

"You're telling me that you're due for a tetanus shot...but you don't really want it?"

He flashed a smile at her. "Yes, ma'am."

"So...maybe I should ask our nurse to help me?" She glanced over her shoulder at Max, who was standing by the file cabinets behind the desk. He flexed his muscles and managed a scowl that was more caricature than fierce.

"No, ma'am. I'm just letting you know that sometimes I get a little woozy." He handed over his completed health history. "I've seen a few too many needles in my time."

She motioned him to follow her down to the first exam room, where she weighed him, then had him sit on the edge of the exam table so she could take his blood pressure and listen to his heart.

"Anything else you want to discuss, other than an overdue tetanus?"

"No, ma'am."

She glanced down at his history, then looked up at him. "Looks like you've been healthy as a horse, other than a mild lead toxicity as a child. I see it was successfully treated, though. Your heart and lungs sound perfect, Mr. Ritter."

Max walked into the room with a loaded syringe, tactfully circling behind the exam table as he would have if there'd been a child in the room, and handed it to her. He waited until she'd delivered the booster, then quietly left.

"So…are you okay?" she said, checking Ethan's skin color and pulse.

"Man, you're good." He rubbed his arm and smiled. "Didn't feel a thing."

She laughed. "Now I know you're kidding, because tetanus toxoid *burns*."

"I hear you have Jim Baxter's horses," he said as he rolled down his sleeve and buttoned his shirt. "He was a good friend of mine."

After growing up in the Dallas area, the grapevine in this small town still surprised and delighted her. "Now, how did you know that?"

"I bought a load of hay this past week from Miranda Wright. We all felt bad when Jim died, and she was real glad his horses have gone back to their old home. Those horses meant everything to him."

"They'll have the best of care, I promise. My son is just thrilled about having his own horse."

"I'm a trainer, so give me a call if you have any problems with them. Jim would've wanted them to be secure in a good home, so I sure won't charge you." He stood and accepted the billing form she'd completed. "I'm one of the homesteaders, too. My place is just a few miles from yours."

They shook hands. "Nice to meet you, neighbor. The Home Free program is an incredible opportunity, isn't it?"

"It is, though not everyone..." He hesitated, as if debating how much to say, then his doubtful expression cleared and he simply gave her a friendly nod. "Nice meeting you."

After cleaning up the exam room, she went out to the front desk. "Any word from Dr. Lou?"

Max shook his head. "Not since she called at nine. I guess that baby is taking its own sweet time in coming." He chuckled as he followed her eyes to the clock. "And you-know-who is due here in five minutes."

"I'm sure he'll be thrilled." Kristin rolled her eyes. "He not only dislikes me personally, but I'm sure he thinks a P.A. is second-best. Fortunately, I've got the cardiologist's report and recommendations here. That's what the doctor would have discussed with him, anyway."

"Good luck. From what I hear, the guy is quite a piece of work. Down at the barbershop, the guys were saying something about favors and bribes— they even implied he has cronies in the local bank, and has been able to influence the outcome of loan applications."

She didn't doubt it for a minute. "Really."

"One old guy warned me to watch out, because Clint is really bitter about the homestead program buying up ranch land he wanted for himself. But what's he going to do? My loan went through, and—"

The front door of the clinic opened with a tinkling of bells, and the man himself walked in, his face a grim mask. Dressed in a perfectly tailored dark suit, crisp white shirt and dark burgundy tie, he looked more ready for a senate committee meeting than a small-town clinic, where the staff wore jeans and running shoes with their uniform tops.

"I hope the doctor's ready, because I don't have time to wait," he announced, looking past Kristin to Max.

"The doctor isn't actually here yet. She's delivering a baby in San Antone," Kristin said. "I have your reports from the cardiologist, though. I can go over them with you and get you set up with the correct prescriptions."

He halted halfway across the waiting room, his jaw working. "I made an appointment with the doctor, and that's who I expect to see."

"She should be here within a few hours. Otherwise, if you want to reschedule she won't be back here for two weeks." Kristin flipped to that page in the appointment book. "That's the twenty-fourth of September."

"Forget it, then." He turned on his heel to leave.

"No—wait," she insisted. "You need to hear what's in the report, and you definitely need to be on the recommended prescriptions. The cardiologist's notes are adamant."

He wavered.

"Please. Just come on back. It will only take a few minutes." Thankful the waiting room was empty, she added, "He believes you're at high risk for a heart attack. This appointment isn't something you should put off."

Muttering something under his breath, Clint gestured sharply. "Fine," he snapped. "Let's get this over with."

Kristin led him into the doctor's private office, figuring he'd be more comfortable there. She waved him toward a chair and took a seat behind the desk, where she withdrew the new cardiology reports from Clint's medical folder. "Your old records from Austin show that you've had long-standing heart failure. You were put on a couple of medications, and the doctor wanted you to come in every two months so he could check your blood pressure and heart. The letter he sent us says he hasn't seen you in over a year."

Clearly bored, Clint picked at an imaginary piece of lint on his sleeve.

"Your cholesterol is 345, your triglycerides are over 400. In addition, your latest EKG shows that your heart failure is getting worse. I imagine you find yourself out of breath climbing stairs, and that there's increased swelling in your ankles."

When he didn't respond, she read the cardiologist's report aloud. "He wants you to have a cath done, the sooner the better, and he wants you to make an appointment with him—or your former cardiologist."

She slid a stack of four prescriptions and a referral slip across the desk. "I've written these out already, so you just need to take them to the pharmacy and have them filled. I'd suggest you do it today. Any questions?"

He reluctantly fingered the papers, then grabbed them and stuffed them in his suit pocket as he stood.

"Look," she said, fighting to keep her voice level. "I know we have a history. I know you don't like me, and that's okay. But you need to follow through on this for the sake of your family—if you want to be around for them."

That must have hit a chord, because he flashed

her a look of pure venom. "I hear you were at the ranch last week."

"Twice, actually."

"Then you really don't listen very well. I told you to stay away from my family. You weren't good enough for my son before, and none of that has changed. You hear?"

She reined in a flash of temper. "Not good enough?"

"Think of the tabloids," he scoffed. "The way they trashed some of the more free-spirited presidential brothers, over the years."

"You placed more importance on some sleazy journalism than on your own son's *happiness?*"

"My son, married to the daughter of a ne'er-do-well? A drunk who went bankrupt and couldn't keep a job? The political damage would've been immeasurable, and it would've embarrassed this entire family."

"Yet you hired my father anyway. Obviously he was a better man than you say."

"No. I hired him years later to give him a chance, and he just proved I was right in the first place about him. He was a drunk, and he was incompetent."

"My father might've tipped a few with his friends, but he was no alcoholic. And it wasn't his fault that the drought hit or that cattle prices fell. A lot of people in the area suffered."

"But *they* weren't trying to weasel into my family."

"Weasel? You probably can't relate, but your son and I actually loved each other. It had nothing to do with his family or his money."

"True love—or true greed?" Clint's face darkened with anger. "You certainly left in a hurry when I told you that I'd disown him if he defied me. That, my dear, says it all."

"I...didn't want him to lose everything because of me."

"Right," he snarled. "And because of you he defied me anyway. I lost my son."

"Lost him? You *disowned* him. It was your decision to slam the door. Otherwise, he might've come back after a few years in the service."

"You have no idea of the damage you've caused." Clint shoved his chair back and swept out of the room. The air still vibrated with his anger after he was gone.

She leaned back in her chair, suddenly exhausted.

She'd heard him all right, and still remembered every word, every threat he'd made all those years ago. Because she had believed him, she'd walked away from the only true love she'd ever had.

And nothing in her life had ever been the same again.

THE REST OF THE DAY grew busier by the minute. Flu. A broken arm. Pneumonia. A ranch hand with a severe laceration and a burn after wrestling a husky calf during branding.

Dr. Lou showed up at noon, which helped, but they still didn't finish until after five-thirty.

Cody, who'd stayed after school for football practice, and had been dropped off at the clinic at five by Trevor's wife, was far more subdued about the wait than he usually was.

"Come on, honey," Kristin said as she shouldered her bag and headed for the door. "I'll bet you're famished."

"I guess."

"Maybe we should stop at the DQ for some cheeseburgers and malts. What do you think, are you hungry enough?" He just nodded.

Even after several talks about the incident at the Four Aces, he'd refused Donna's invitation to go back there again and hadn't even wanted to go riding yesterday, which added to Kristin's worry.

At the DQ, they settled at a table under a brightly striped umbrella with hot fudge malts, cheeseburgers and an extra large basket of onion rings.

Cody dug into the onion rings, while Kristin savored her juicy cheeseburger and idly surveyed the jumble of businesses on the edge of town. A parts store, a feed store…and a little farther out, she could see just the top of the sign for Buddy's Auto Shop.

She'd wanted to get out there for a week now, but the clinic's schedule had filled rapidly and Buddy's hours were erratic. He'd been closed every time she managed to get out there at five. But maybe...

She stood and shaded her eyes as she scanned the low hill behind the businesses flanking the main highway out of town. Perhaps she couldn't actually talk to Buddy himself, but even from here she could make out haphazard rows of old vehicles parked inside a high wooden fence on the slope behind Buddy's shop. Surely he wouldn't mind if she just walked back there and tried to peek through the fence.

"I've got an idea, Cody. Let's finish our supper on the way home, okay? I have one stop to make first, and then we'll get home early enough to ride for a while."

He nodded obediently and gathered up his burger and malt. When she pulled into a shady spot in front of Buddy's, he looked at her with astonishment. "We're stopping *here?*"

She rolled both windows down partway, then hit the locks as she stepped out of the truck. "Stay inside with the doors locked. I'll just be a minute."

"But they're closed."

"I know. I just want to check out the old cars in

back." He appeared intrigued with *that* idea, but if he started asking questions, she wouldn't be able to answer them. Not just yet, anyway. "Finish those onion rings before I get back, or we'll be fighting over them," she teased.

She rounded the building, avoiding barrels and greasy puddles. "Hello—anyone here?"

She heard a dog barking, but no one appeared. She skirted the rusted hulks of several old tractors and stacks of various parts and pieces, and warily made her way through the tall weeds to the fenced enclosure out back.

Something rustled past her shoes and she jumped back with a hand at her mouth, imagining snakes and rats. Mosquitoes swarmed about her face as she crossed a low damp spot, where a foul stench rose from rusted drums filled with stagnant rainwater and the iridescent shimmer of discarded oil.

Batting at the persistent insects, she hurried to higher ground.

The fence was a good ten feet tall or more, constructed of solid wood planks, but it was an old one. She slowly moved up the hill, stopping wherever she found warped or broken boards that afforded a glimpse inside. She surveyed the first row of vehicles, then the next.

Many of the vehicles had been parted out down to the barest skeleton. Most looked as if they'd been there for aeons and were becoming part of the landscape, with sagebrush and twisted cedars growing up through the gaping holes where engines and hoods were missing.

The sun-warmed smell of old oil and rubber made her eyes burn. She'd just reached the halfway point and had steadied herself with a hand on the fence when a dog burst out of the shadows barking furiously, its jaws snapping at the fence not inches away from her.

Startled, she cried out and fell back a step, breathing hard as a rush of adrenaline shot through her.

A second later, a middle-aged man in jeans, an oil-stained shirt and a ball cap strode into view. He didn't look friendly.

"Down, Rascal," he commanded. Its tail wagging now, the black Lab backed away, though its eyes never left Kristin's face.

"I…I was hoping to find a particular vehicle," Kristin said faintly.

"Most people come during business hours," he retorted. "Those who come out here alone are usually up to no good."

"I—I've been trying to get here during your business hours, but I work at the clinic in town and you're always closed after five."

"The front door is closed," he corrected her. "Most folks around here know that I'm usually in back, working till late." He studied her. "What are you looking for?"

"My father's pickup. A '67 Chevy that rolled over just about eighteen months ago. Sheriff Montgomery said it was towed here. Are you Buddy?"

"Yep." The man visibly relaxed. "But it won't do you no good to go looking, there wasn't much of anything usable left on that truck. It got crushed and hauled a long time back."

Kristin's heart fell. "You're sure."

"Sorry, but that probably ain't how you want to remember your daddy anyway, is it?"

She looked past him to the rows of vehicles she hadn't searched yet. There might even be some vehicles she couldn't see, from this side of the fence, and that thought gave her renewed hope. "But—"

"Come on down to the office." He smiled kindly. "I got to keep book work on what comes and goes out of here, and everything gets tagged with a number. I'll show you, so you don't keep thinking that ole truck is here. I'll meet you out front."

She made her way back down the hill to the open door of the shop, where Buddy stood. "Just one more minute," she called out to Cody as she passed.

He hopped out of the truck to join her. "This

looks like a cool place. How come I couldn't go see those cars with you?"

"There was nothing to see, really." She hesitated before letting him come along into the cramped office. A badly crumpled vehicle might have raised frightening images for him, but documents would have much less emotional impact. She curved an arm around his shoulders for a quick hug. "I just wanted to find out about your grandfather Nate's old truck."

Obviously not yet in the computer age, Buddy lifted a big ledger from a shelf jammed with small auto parts, a well-stained coffee mug and some old rags.

He flipped through the pages, then turned the book around for her to read an entry written in an awkward, looping scrawl.

She held her breath as she read it, then sighed with disappointment. "You're right. I'm sorry to have bothered you like this."

"And I'm sorry I couldn't be more help. I knew Nate real well, and I kept that ole truck around longer than I should have just because it was his." Buddy closed the book and rested his grease-stained hands on it, as if saying goodbye to his old friend. "I'm real sorry about your loss."

CHAPTER TWELVE

RYAN LED JAZZ over to the electric walker, snapped one of the dangling lead chains to the colt's halter and gave him a congratulatory pat on the neck. "Good job, fella."

Outside the enclosure, he flipped a switch to start the rotation of the octopus-like metal arms that radiated from the central motor. The colt obediently set off at a slow walk around the circular path. In a half hour, he'd be cool and dry, ready to turn out into a corral for the night with his kindergarten-level buddies, who were all in training, too.

Ryan shouldered the colt's cotton lead rope and started for the tack room, feeling better physically than he had in a long time.

Months of surgeries and therapy had put him back on his feet again. Leaving behind the wheelchair, and then his cane, had been victories hard won.

He knew he'd never forget the horrors of what he'd seen and done in the service. His shoulder and knee might never be right again. But on the back of a young horse, he'd felt truly *alive*...as if he was finally able to decide his own future without the shackles of permanent disability holding him back.

He'd stepped into the tack room when he heard a soft rustle, and the presence of another person suddenly registered. He turned back into the darkened aisle.

Partway down, almost hidden in the shadows, a tall, thin figure stood at one of the stalls, petting the nose of the horse inside. She turned. "Hello, dear."

A multitude of emotions surfaced—surprise, delight, a touch of irritation at seeing her standing so casually here as if she'd never left. "Mother."

She sauntered forward, all angular sophistication and grace, her salt-and-pepper hair swinging in an oblique cut at her jaw. Her rough-woven cream sweater and beige slacks looked more Houston than Homestead. "It's been a long time, dear." She rested her slender fingers on his shoulders, brushed a cool kiss against his cheek, then leaned back to survey him. "You look marvelous."

Marvelous wasn't the way he felt right now, but he returned her smile. "As do you."

Her face seemed to fall for a split second, then she rallied, a conspiratorial smile deepening the feathery wrinkles at her eyes. "I do believe I surprised your father this morning, the old goat. I probably took two years off his life."

"I'm not sure he'd want to give you that pleasure."

"Score," she said lightly. "Although it might surprise you to hear that I really don't wish him any harm."

"I remember. You were the best of friends." He laughed. "As long as there were at least three hundred miles between you."

"Divorce was the right choice," she agreed. She fingered the heavy gold chain at her neck. "For the two of us at least, but not for you boys. I'll always regret some of the decisions made back then."

He doubted that. Lydia Gallagher had been a free spirit, a strong woman with a streak of stubborn independence that matched Clint's, and they'd been like gasoline and flame. The wonder was they'd stayed together long enough to produce three children.

"What brings you here?" He smiled. "Or do you come out often, now?"

"You *are* joking." She pulled a face. "I see the boys, of course, and Trevor's family, but I choose to not overstress your father by arriving when he's in town, and I always stay with Trevor. I believe Clint prefers it that way, and so do I."

The Gallagher home had been a shining example of marital bliss—and where it could lead, if everything went wrong. Armed camps. Careful awareness of enemy lines. At least with the Gallagher money, there hadn't been the financial devastation of divorce he'd seen in the lives of some of his buddies in the service.

Long separations and the continual stress of knowing a loved one was facing constant danger certainly took its toll.

"But you're staying here this time?" he asked. When she nodded he raised a brow, imagining the silence and solitude of the big old house erupting into World War III.

"I heard you were here, and I knew I had to come. It's been so many years since we spent any time together." Her breezy veneer seemed to crack just a little. "I know I wasn't very attentive when you were tykes, and that your father and I can't undo how we handled things. But I'd like a chance to be with you for a while."

She studied him, the faint hope in her eyes making him feel as if perhaps he should hug her, though his first impulse was to shake her hand. The awkward moment lengthened, trapping him as if his boots had been glued to the floor, until she released him with a light laugh.

"Don't worry, dear. I don't intend to pounce like your Great Aunt Flora. Remember her—with the jangling bracelets and head scarves? She used to smother you with hugs when you were a toddler."

Lydia rested her hand on Ryan's cheek. "I think I'll go back up to the house and turn in early. I'm sure you must have a thousand things to do out here." With a flutter of her fingertips she strolled out of the barn, thin and graceful, and as coolly unapproachable as ever.

Her dry humor was still there. The flinty attitude. But something wasn't quite right, and Ryan just hoped that his premonition was wrong.

MINDFUL OF HIS ACHING shoulder, Ryan lifted yet another battered cardboard box from the floor of the closet in the office and dropped it on the desk in a haze of dust. He kept thinking back to what Kristin had said last Saturday.

What was it like, losing your father and wondering if his was a wrongful death? Coming back to a town where rumors still flew about his association with a man many mistrusted or downright feared?

Ryan had grown up on the Four Aces, but he hadn't been deaf to the whispers and the cautious, sidelong glances. Kids had talked at school, repeated what parents said.

Most thought Clint had risen to political power through carefully placed cronies and well-spent money. No one doubted that he could still call in favors and influence the future of anyone he chose. And Nate Cantrell, who'd been an oc-

casional employee and who'd also been part of
several minor business schemes, had been tarred
with the same brush.

The hurt in Cody's eyes at that football game a
week ago had touched Ryan. Having an absentee
father like Ted had to be tough enough, and now
Cody was aware of the ill will against his grandfather, as well. Poor kid.

Ryan lifted a dozen rubber band-bound manila
folders out of the box on the desk, stuffed with
yellowed receipts, notes scrawled on scraps of
paper and bank statements. There hadn't been
any organization to the previous box he'd gone
through, and this one looked just as bad.

He fired up the computer and launched Excel,
then painstakingly went through each slip of
paper, recording equipment, feed, supplies, services, sales receipts. He separated them into the
cattle or horse operations where possible.

By the time he got to the March boxes, he'd
developed an uneasy feeling that there were in-
consistencies. By the time he got to May, he was
sure of it. He printed off what he'd completed for
the most recent twelve months and what he'd done
so far for the year before, then went through each
bank statement, each bill and receipt.

None of it made sense.

There was almost no consistency in the numbers from last year until now. Expenditures were

far higher—or missing altogether—and some goods and services had been added in the past year that had never appeared before, from what he could see.

In disgust, Ryan tossed a stack of files back in the box and abandoned the office to watch Trevor and Garrett working some young colts in the outdoor arena.

Garrett glanced at Ryan but kept working his mount in smaller and smaller circles at a lope.

Trevor jogged over to the side of the arena, eased his horse to a stop and shook out some slack in the reins. "What's up?"

"I'll trade you jobs," Ryan said. "I'd much rather work a colt than wade through the mess in that office."

"It's my fault, much as anyone's, I guess. I should have been in the office more." Guilt flashed in his brother's eyes. "Oscar was always grumbling about how much there was to do, but I always figured it would all get done, somehow. When Nate came he seemed so much more efficient that I was just relieved to make him responsible. Put me on a horse or a tractor, and I know what I'm doing. A computer—good luck."

"How did y'all ever handle quarterly taxes the past few years?"

"Leland, Clint...it all worked out, I guess."

But a tax audit now would be a nightmare… and the possibility of fines, late taxes and the levy of interest on overdue payments could deliver a crushing blow to a ranch that already appeared to be on shaky ground. "Did you talk to the accountant who tried to sort this out—the one who discovered the embezzlement?"

"Briefly." Trevor tipped his hat back and rested a forearm across his saddle horn. "But that was last spring, when I was gone for six weeks. Donna and I were hauling the new stud and some younger stock to the bigger quarter horse shows."

"I'm finding boxes of old records. Haphazard filing…"

"Yeah, that's what the accountant said. What you see is how he found it—and he was plumb irritated, too. I hear he stayed at the ranch for two weeks longer than he'd planned. He finally said there was so much missing documentation that he could only guess."

"I've read his report. It was just what you and Leland said. Huge losses and the lost or altered records were probably a cover-up."

Trevor stroked the sweaty neck of the buckskin. "We got what we deserved, I guess…but I swear, I always thought Nate was a good guy. Had a run of tough luck over the years maybe, but he always seemed like a straight shooter."

"I feel bad about that grandson of his."

Trevor's jaw tightened. "I had a long talk with Hayden afterward. He knows better than to talk about ranch business with his buddies, so there won't be any gossip about Cody's grandpa at school."

"Cody's a new kid on the block around here, with a dad who's a jerk and a grandfather who was probably an embezzler. What kind of male role models does he have? I think we should try to help him a little."

Trevor nodded thoughtfully. "We can help the boys patch up their differences, maybe…and try getting them together more often."

"Right."

A corner of Trevor's mouth lifted. "And that would have nothing to do with Cody's pretty momma."

"I'm thinking about the boy, not her," Ryan retorted.

"Riiiight."

Trevor's Texas drawl filled the word with implications Ryan didn't want to think about. But he couldn't deny that Kristin had lurked at the edge of his thoughts 24-7 since he'd arrived in Homestead. Not to mention for the past fifteen years.

He'd long since realized he wasn't ever going to marry, though. Not with the kind of career he had, the kind of risks he took every day. The divorce rate among his fellow Rangers was astronomical, and seeing firsthand what a bitter breakup did to the children, he would never take the risk.

Maybe Kristin brought back memories of when he'd believed differently. It didn't matter. Soon he'd be leaving for the East Coast, while she was obviously settling in for the long haul on her homesteaded land.

But she and her son deserved so much more than a legacy of lost trust and the shame of Nate's misdeeds. Had he *really* stolen the money? How could anyone be sure, when the ranch records were so flawed? If Clint's failures meant Nate was still taking the rap for something he hadn't done...

On his way back to the office, Ryan set his jaw and made a silent vow to himself.

Before he left Texas, he was going to uncover the truth about what had happened here over the past few years. Perhaps Oscar had been the one who'd taken off with the money, or perhaps the losses were simply the result of massive incompetence.

Given Clint's history, it wasn't beyond belief there might've been other reasons for that money to disappear.

Kristin believed in her father's innocence, and even Trevor had doubted his guilt. Whatever the answer was, Ryan was going to find it.

CLINT PACED THROUGH his spacious bedroom with a highball in his hand and a half-empty bottle of bourbon on the dresser, his shirt collar unbuttoned, his tie loose.

He'd had Trevor fly him back to Austin in the ranch helicopter for the afternoon, where he'd met with his campaign manager to discuss next year's election. After a late dinner and a few drinks with some of his cronies, he and Trevor had flown home at about midnight.

It had been a long, difficult day. He was exhausted. But he already knew that sleep would elude him, just as it had the night before. Lydia was here in the house somewhere, though he hadn't seen her since that first chance meeting.

The thought made him want to smash his glass into the fireplace.

Twenty-five years. Twenty-five years of solitude. Peace. Utter control. And now she was back.

He stalked to the king-size bed, with its cool sheets that were turned down at a precise angle each night by Adelfa. Fresh, crisp sheets every night. He considered, then discarded the possibility that he might be tired enough to sleep anyway...so he jerked open the sliding-glass doors and stepped out into the crisp night air.

An ancient live oak shaded the enclosed courtyard by day. At night, it filtered lacy moonlight onto the stone walkways and flowering bushes, the wrought-iron benches. He tipped back the glass and finished off his bourbon, welcoming the smooth liquid fire down his throat as he headed for a bench at the base of the oak.

Where, with any luck, perhaps he could sit and doze.

It took him a moment to realize he wasn't alone.

"We used to come out here together," Lydia said as she stepped out of the shadows. "Remember?"

Her throaty chuckle reminded him of all the times they'd kissed out here under the moonlight. The days when they'd been young and impassioned, their verbal battles sometimes escalating beyond anything he had the energy for now. He turned to go, but her soft laughter stopped him.

"We were all wrong for each other, weren't we?" She stepped closer, her white shimmery robe glowing in the moonlight. "A disaster from day one...yet we sure didn't go wrong with those boys."

"Oh?" He scoffed. "Tell me where we went right—no wait a minute, you weren't around."

She didn't answer for a long moment. "I might have been, except..."

"Right. The gallery. Your...your...friend."

"Harris?" She sank onto a bench. "You never believed me. You just assumed."

"And it hardly matters, does it," Clint said flatly.

He rolled his shoulders irritably. "When are you leaving?"

"Really, Clint." Her voice held the same hint of contempt that had driven his fury years ago.

It drew the line between her wealthy upbringing and his as a dirt farmer's son.

Her East Coast education and his from a state university.

Her old money had been his stake in this ranch, his start in politics. Though she'd never said a word, she'd still managed to convey her utter boredom with his dreams.

"I'm long past these games," he growled. "I'm turning in."

"Where you'll sleep as well as I have, no doubt."

"What do you want?" He turned, intending to stare her down, but instead found himself taking in her ghostly pale face. The deep hollows under her cheekbones. "Lydia, you look terrible."

That earned another soft laugh. "A woman can never be too thin, Clint. Fashion is *everything*. On the other hand, a man can be far too rude."

"Some of us just don't care." He sighed heavily, knowing she was the one person on earth who would defy him at every turn, who would call him on every last mistake. And she *never* yielded the last word in an argument.

"Sad, isn't it?" Her voice sounded wistful. "We should have been such an amazing team.

Now here we are, nearly sixty, and we still can't manage five minutes of conversation. I wish…it had been different. For us. For our boys."

He didn't know how to respond to that.

"Don't worry, dear. I haven't come to stay. I plan to leave in a few days for a buying trip in New York, then hope to get back here again while Ryan is still around." She played with the top button of her robe. "Once he takes off again, we may not see him for years and I think it's long past time to be mending fences."

"That ought to keep you busy," Clint snapped.

"So you've made no mistakes," she said mildly. "You know, I used to think that failing memory was a curse for the elderly. Now, I think it's probably a blessing, because it gives peace of mind that some of them don't deserve. Good night, darling. Sleep well."

She rose and drifted into the shadows toward the opposite wing of the house. A moment later he heard the soft slide of a glass door, and the snick of a lock.

The tension in his chest eased. He crossed the courtyard for his room, where he felt the weight of exhaustion settling back over him. This time, he thought he might be able to sleep.

But long after he settled in, he lay staring at the ceiling. Lydia was a master at subtle criticism.

He'd never once won an argument with her, but she'd also been more than fair.

She could have destroyed the Four Aces and his budding political career by taking what was rightfully hers in the divorce, under Texas law. Instead, she'd scoffed at her insistent lawyers and had accepted just enough to put herself through college. She'd earned an art degree—something Clint had thought useless as snowshoes on a long-horn. Yet she'd made her way in the world very well.

Past mistakes. He remembered his own all too well. There was no fix for them, not after all this time. And there was no question about ever reaching a friendly accord.

But maybe…he needed to mend a few fences, as well.

CHAPTER THIRTEEN

AT THE SOUND of a vehicle pulling up, Kristin put the last of the supper dishes into the dishwasher, rinsed her hands and went to the front porch.

Ryan stepped out of his truck and grinned at her, his thumbs hooked in the front pockets of his Levi's. "Is he ready?"

Behind her, she could hear feet thundering down the stairs. A second later, Cody burst out the door and skidded to an ungainly stop at her side. "I think so," she said dryly.

Cody gave her a quick hug and raced off for the passenger's side of the truck. Through the front window, she could see Hayden bowed over something that had his full attention—probably the new Nintendo DSi that Cody coveted and she couldn't afford.

"Thanks for helping smooth things over between the boys," Kristin murmured. "It means a lot to Cody to have a friend here."

"Trevor handled it, really. Hayden promised he'd never refer to Cody's grandpa again, and he promised to apologize. After that, I think the boys mostly patched things up on their own."

"Still, you've been so good about getting the boys together to play. Should I pick up Cody again around six?"

Ryan tipped his head toward the cab of his truck. "You could come over now, if you've got time. I could bring you both home."

"Oh. Well…" She fought the urge to smooth back her hair. "I could drive over and save you the trip."

His grin deepened. "No bother. Just grab a jacket and come on. I'd bet the boys would like you to see how good they are now. I think we've got some NFL champs on the way."

She'd once worried that Cody was developing a serious case of hero worship, and she hadn't been far wrong. The boy talked about Ryan, the ranch and Hayden's cool dad from dawn to dusk, always with a touch of awe and envy that saddened her.

He'd also made some not-too-subtle hints about her getting involved with Ryan, and for that reason she'd been taking special care to keep a casual distance between them. But now, with Cody looking back at her, she could hardly refuse.

"Hold on just a minute." In the house, she caught sight of herself as she passed the front hall mirror. *You hardly have to worry about any unwanted attention.* Her hair was escaping its ponytail, her T-shirt splotched with water from the pots and pans she'd just washed in the sink. *In fact, you look pathetic.*

Ditching the T-shirt, she pulled on an emerald sweater. Considered it in her dresser mirror. Jerked it off and decided on a crimson cashmere wannabe instead. Tried scraping her hair into a knot on top of her head, disgusted when the silky strands slithered right out of the clip.

In defeat she simply ran a brush through her hair and let it fall straight to her shoulders, slapped on some lip gloss and mascara and headed out to Ryan's truck with a denim jacket slung over her shoulders.

Cody rolled his eyes as he and Hayden shifted out of the front seat of the crew cab pickup. "What took you so long?"

She ruffled his hair as he climbed in. "Five minutes, sweetie. When you get old enough to date, you'll be cooling your heels for *hours*."

Both boys groaned as they fastened their seat belts, then bent together over the handheld video game. She closed the back door, then slid into the front seat. "This is awfully nice of you, Ryan. Thanks."

"No problem." His gaze stayed on her for a moment, then he cleared his throat and shifted the truck into gear. "I can only stand office work so long, and then I have to get outside. The boys give me a good excuse."

"Are you enjoying your time at the ranch?"

He steered around several of the bigger potholes in a low spot of the road. "It's definitely been interesting."

"How much time do you have left?"

He rolled his left shoulder, perhaps unconsciously testing it in response. "Thanksgiving. No longer."

"And then?"

"I'll go back." He glanced at her and added, "Seventy-fifth Ranger Regiment, Third Battalion. Fort Benning."

She wondered if he knew how often he massaged his damaged knee, or that his skin paled if he took an uneven step. Or if he realized there were dark shadows under his eyes, telltale signs of all he'd been through. "What will you do, exactly?"

"Rejoin my platoon." His jaw tensed. "Or... I could end up as a trainer."

Obviously not his first choice, given the grim set of his mouth.

There was nothing between them now other than a tentative, growing friendship, but the thought of her living in Homestead and him in Georgia—if not on the other side of the world— saddened her.

"The boys will miss you."

"I hadn't been back for a long time. Now, I'll probably make the trip whenever I have leave." He glanced at Hayden in the rearview mirror. "I've been missing too much."

When they pulled to a stop by the barns at the Four Aces, the boys piled out and raced for a football lying in the grass, tackling each other and squealing as they wrestled like puppies over the ball. Friends now, they'd had dinner at each other's houses, and last Saturday she'd taken them to a matinee at the old cheap-seats theater in Homestead—a reclamation project of yet another newcomer to town.

The difference in Cody's attitude was amazing.

Ryan jogged over to the boys and gestured for them to move out into a wide triangle from him, then they began passing the football. His own throws so gentle, they were almost in slow motion.

An unfamiliar sense of completion settled over Kristin as she moved to a bench under a live oak and watched. Cody and Hayden missed as many catches as they made. Their throws fell short or went wide, but they were better than they'd been, and with every effort Ryan's deep voice called out encouragement and praise.

Cody needed this so much. Even from fifty yards away, she could see him beam in response to such unfamiliar praise from a man he respected.

Ted, she remembered bitterly, would have offered up caustic remarks and cursed after a few failed throws. Then he would have spiked the ball in frustration on his way back to the house.

Leaning against the back of the bench, she glanced toward the massive Gallagher home. An elegant woman stepped out the front door with a small suitcase on wheels and trundled it to the back of a pearl-gray Lincoln. She stowed it in the trunk, then climbed behind the wheel.

The car slowly made its way down the circular drive to the parking lot, lingered next to Ryan for a moment, then both Ryan and the driver looked at Kristin. Seconds later, the car purred over to Kristin, and the driver rolled down her window.

"I don't believe we've met, dear. I'm Ryan's mother."

Kristin rose and walked over to greet her. Long ago, she'd heard stories about the callous woman who'd brazenly walked out of the house one day without a second thought for her young boys. The woman in the car bore no resemblance to the image Kristin had formed.

Thin, her silver hair twisted into a sophisticated chignon, she had the elegant bone structure and subtly perfect makeup of someone who'd come from wealth and knew the value of understatement.

With a beige sweater knotted over her shoulders

and a cascade of gold geometric shapes dangling at her ears, she might have been ready for lunch at a private club. But the warmth of her smile was in surprising contrast to her appearance and bearing.

Kristin shook her hand briefly, noted the almost skeletal fragility of the woman. *Too thin.* And her skin...at a distance, she'd merely been pale. At close range, she had the cachectic look of someone very ill. "I'm happy to meet you. Are you... still Mrs. Gallagher?"

"Yes. To Clint's everlasting discomfort, I'm sure. In a way, it was always a connection to my children. Though a minor one, to be sure." She laughed as if dismissing her foolishness, but her eyes were sad. "Tell me about yourself, dear. I hear you're a physician's assistant?"

"Yes, ma'am."

"Please, I'm just Lydia. I do love Texas manners, but I'd rather you used my first name." She raised a delicately arched brow. "My son didn't say a word, but a little bird told me that you were here once, a long time ago. Meeting the family, as it were."

"There's nothing between us now." Uncomfortable, Kristin glanced at Ryan's back as he threw the football to Cody. "We're just neighbors. Unexpectedly so."

Smiling faintly, Lydia searched her face. "Then

I shall hope that you become much better friends, dear. I think you might be exactly what he needs."

Kristin choked back a laugh. "You haven't been talking to Clint, then."

"Actually, he's been gone most of the time I've been here. On purpose, I'm sure." She waved a hand toward the house, where just the tips of a helicopter's rotor were visible through the trees. "I heard that thing take off this morning at six. Adelfa said Trevor took him to Austin, and that he'll be gone for several nights."

"While you're here? That's too bad."

"It's *intentional,* my dear. But that's fine. I came to see my boys, anyway." The humor in her eyes faded. "I know about what happened between you and Ryan years ago. I'm sure Clint was completely at fault, and that the old goat probably isn't any happier about you now than he was back then. That man never forgets a grudge."

"But—"

Lydia interrupted her with a lift of her hand. "If—*if* you and Ryan form an attachment, I hope you'll ignore his father and listen to your heart. Clint has already ruined far too many lives with his interference." She shifted the car into Reverse. "Don't give him that power again."

She started backing up, and Kristin jogged to catch up. "Wait—are you coming back?"

"After a trip to New York. I know it will just

brighten up Clint's life all over again." With a musical laugh Lydia waved, backed the car into a deft three-point turn and disappeared down the lane, leaving Kristin to stare after her.

She was nothing like the harridan Kristin had imagined, and now the stories she'd heard rang false. What could have happened to make her leave three children behind? It had been a terrible loss for them then and it was too late to erase the pain now, but someday they all needed to know the truth.

On Friday, Ryan made it till noon before his knee ached too much to sit at the desk any longer...and the prospect of practicing catches and kicks with the two little hooligans made his shoulder throb in anticipation. Regretfully he dialed the number of the clinic.

Max—the nurse who looked as if he could take down the Mafia single-handedly—answered with a cheerful hello, then Kristin came on the line a few minutes later.

"That should work out well," she said, after he explained the reason for his call. "This is Ted's weekend for Cody. He and his wife are coming at five, so we would've been cutting it a little close, anyway."

"Good, then." Though Ryan couldn't imagine

what Cody—or anyone else—would do during an entire weekend with Ted. "I hope they have fun."

The brief silence at the other end of the phone spoke volumes. "I know they'll take good care of him, that he'll be safe. It's not a weekend each month that I look forward to, though. I think Cody would rather be here, and the place will be lonely without him."

He should have murmured something appropriate and then hung up. Instead, he found himself holding the phone a little tighter. "So what do you do when he's gone?"

"Read. Clean. Now, I've got bedrooms to paint and stalls to clean. The excitement is beyond imagining, don't you think?"

"Definitely beyond." He cleared his throat, "I…I'm going to a rodeo this evening. Garrett just took off with his buddies, and he's entered in the bull riding tonight. I told him I'd be there."

"That sounds like fun."

"More than painting? You're sure welcome to come along."

"Um…is that all of you? Trevor and Donna, too? The kids?"

"Just me. Trevor's delivering a show mare to some customers in Houston. His family is going along."

"Oh."

"Don't worry about it. I'm sure you need the extra time at home, and—"

"No—wait. I'll go. I haven't been to a rodeo in years. It sounds great. What time are you leaving?"

"Rodeo starts at seven. I figure it'll take an hour or so to get there and find the rodeo grounds."

"And then you'll want good seats," she teased. "Near the chutes, where all the cowboys eat dirt—except your brother, of course."

"*Especially* my brother. Sooo...five-thirty? Your place?"

"Deal."

After he disconnected, his initial elation faded to much cooler realization.

He found himself looking forward to playing football with the boys because it meant he'd get to see her for a few minutes almost every day. She still appealed to him in every way—even more than she had when they were kids. He'd firmly ignored the urge to ask her out, though, knowing it would create unnecessary complications. She wasn't the type of woman who had casual flings, and he wasn't staying around.

And now he was taking her out on a date. Of sorts.

What on earth had he been thinking?

WHAT ON EARTH was I thinking? Kristin paced her living room after Ted picked up Cody. *I can call*

Ryan and say I'm sick. Or that I've got to...do errands. Or that the horses escaped and I've got to chase them down.

But they were lies, and she'd long ago learned that she was a terrible liar.

She would go on this...this date. She'd be friendly, congenial and appreciative. And then she'd never make the mistake again.

There was too much history between them... too many old feelings lurking just below the surface. Clint's opinion didn't matter, because she already knew that falling for Ryan would set her up for heartbreak, and the last time had been hard enough.

It took six changes of clothes to decide on the right mix of color and not-trying-to-impress-you style. And, after she'd slipped into snug, boot-cut black Levi's and a deep royal blue sweater, she went through three pairs of gold earrings before she found the right fit.

When she met Ryan at her front door, his look of appreciation boosted her anticipation—and her trepidation. Maybe it was a mistake to be going with him tonight, but what harm could come of it? An evening at a rodeo. A leisurely drive.

There was nothing to worry about at all.

CHAPTER FOURTEEN

SHE'D STARTED OUT by sitting a respectable distance away, but midway through the rodeo, Kristin leaned into Ryan to ward off the chilly night air and cradled her cup of hot cocoa and plate of fried chicken, thankful for their warmth.

They sat five rows up, just past the front of the chutes, and all around them, the crowd alternately had cheered and moaned as the events rolled past. Saddle broncs. Team roping. The barrel racers in flashy sequined tops. Bareback broncs. Goat tying for fledgling cowpokes.

During the intermission, she'd been spellbound by the kids riding calves out in the arena.

"A guy told me that the fried chicken concession here is the best in the whole region." Ryan grinned at her. "You oughta eat that before I polish off yours, too."

"Right now, it's keeping my hands warm. Who knew it would be so cold tonight?"

He gave her a nudge. "The weather guy on the radio, for one."

"Aah, but you didn't bring a jacket, either," she

countered. She dug into the fried chicken and sighed blissfully. "This is fantastic. How many people would think of coming to a rodeo for something like this?"

He waved a hand toward the overflow crowd, most of them families with children of all ages. "Them, for starters. I bet a lot of these people come out every time there's a rodeo in town—that line at the food booth still trails out into the parking lot."

She savored another bite. "We were lucky we got here early."

"Hang on to our seats, would you? I'm going behind the chutes to check on Garrett. He should be up pretty soon."

She watched Ryan ease past the others sitting in their row, then make his way down the packed bleachers. Nothing to worry about if she came to this rodeo with him? She'd been dead wrong. Until now, whenever she'd seen him, there'd been other people around—Cody, Hayden, Max—and they'd served as a comfortable buffer that kept interaction superficial.

But tonight... Oh, my.

On the way here, they'd slipped right into the same easy repartee they'd shared back in college, discussing everything from the Dallas Cowboys to the ongoing troubles in the Middle East, from the last book they'd each read to a professor they'd both had for Statistics 101 in college. She'd forgotten how easy Ryan was to talk to…how the hours could just roll past and seem like minutes.

It was all coming back, though. She wished they weren't surrounded by a thousand raucous rodeo fans, because now she longed to find out if other things were the same, as well.

The way he kissed, for instance, cradling her head in his hands as if she were the most precious thing in the world. No one else had ever made her feel that way. Definitely not Ted. Not the few other men she'd tried dating after the divorce, either.

Yep, she was in trouble, yet she and Ryan hadn't so much as exchanged a single, chaste kiss. And probably wouldn't, if his cautious distance was any clue.

He'd rested a courteous hand at the small of her back as they made their way through the crowd. Draped an arm across her shoulders to tell her something while they'd waited in that interminable chicken line with loudspeakers blaring overhead.

But he hadn't made a move otherwise, and it was for the best.

A hefty woman, her four kids and skinny husband squeezed past, stepping on Kristin's toes with murmurs of apology and spilling several pieces of popcorn down her scoop neck sweater.

Once they made it past, she surreptitiously tried to retrieve the popcorn.

"You okay with that?"

Embarrassed, she looked up into Ryan's twinkling eyes. "Thanks, yes."

He tossed her a bulky plastic sack. "Check this out."

Surprised, she retrieved the last piece of popcorn, tore open the package, and lifted out a lightweight Western down jacket, in deep garnet red. "Oh, my," she breathed. "This is *beautiful.*"

"Try it on."

It had to have cost a good hundred dollars or more. "I—it's gorgeous, but I just can't accept it—and I don't have this kind of money along."

"Consider it a gift. If you keep shivering, you're going to end up shaking us both right off of these bleachers."

"But—"

"Consider it a very *belated* gift, then." His eyes darkened. "I remember when I wished I could buy you the moon, and I could barely afford hamburgers and malts. This is from the boy back then."

"I…well…" She faltered, then finally accepted it. "I'll pay you back next month, I promise."

"Don't. I—"

"Ladies and Gentlemen!" The announcer's voice rose to a crescendo, the crowd cheering in response. "The event you've been waiting for all night. The event that means life or death in eight seconds for these rough, tough, crazy cowboys—and the rodeo clowns who risk their lives to save them. Folks, it's *bull riding*. On deck now, in Chute 3, we have..."

Ryan helped Kristin into the jacket, then wedged onto the seat next to her. "I found Garrett, and I tried to talk him out of this. Nearly got a black eye in the process."

"He's not good at it? Or are you just a worried big brother?"

"He's already got some sort of injury. He's taking a big chance."

"I'll keep my fingers crossed for him, then." Kristin craned her neck to see over the tall cowboy hat in front of her.

A small black bull took one jump out of Chute 3 then dived into a hard spin to the right. Two rodeo clowns closed in, their entire focus on the wildly bucking bull and the rider who was tipping precariously to the left. In a flash he was airborne. The buzzer sounded two seconds later.

Five other cowboys came out, but only two made it to the buzzer and both scored low.

"There he is. He's up next," Ryan said pointing toward the chutes. "And according to the rodeo program, he's got a serious draw. Jackhammer."

Her attention riveted on Chute 5, she barely

heard the announcer's spiel about the bull's bucking history.

The bull—a massive red roan—reared in the chute and tried to crawl over the top of the gate. Garrett stepped off onto the rail until he settled, then eased back onto the bull's broad, heavily muscled back. He took a quick wrap of bull rope, nodding to the gate man. The gate swung wide. The bull exploded into the arena with unleashed power that brought Kristin and the rest of the crowd to their feet.

Jackhammer tore into a fast spin to the left, then reversed gears and took a high, twisting leap to the right, its bell jangling and hooves slamming into the earth with jaw-rattling force as it dodged back to the left. Stumbled.

Then crashed into the row of closed chute gates with Garrett somewhere beneath it.

The clowns both raced forward, inches from the front of the bull as it staggered to its feet, shook its horns and spun back to slam Garrett against the chute once, then twice before losing interest.

Two mounted ring men raced over and herded the bull out of the arena. The gate men rushed to Garrett's side, and the medic arrived seconds later.

Stunned, Kristin hurried after Ryan as he flew

down the risers to the arena, vaulted over the fence and ran to Garrett.

But even after those endless seconds, Garrett wasn't moving.

BY THE TIME the ambulance had loaded Garrett, he was half-conscious and talking, his blood pressure stable, but no one could be sure of just how much damage he'd incurred.

Ryan's face was impassive as they followed the ambulance to a nearby hospital.

"You tried to stop him," Kristin said. "That's all you could do. He's a grown man, making his own decisions."

"Stupid ones," Ryan bit out. "He's throwing his life away on this. From what I hear, even his rodeo buddies have tried to make him back off on the bulls."

"He doesn't see that for himself?"

"He's cocky, he's young. Thinks he owns the world, and the bull riders are the stars of the rodeo."

"And that kind of thinking could get him killed." Kristin laid a hand on Ryan's arm. "At least you were here tonight."

"To pick up the pieces?" He gave her a brief glance. "He won't thank me for it. He's run wild most of his life, and has refused to answer to anyone. This won't be the end of it, I'm sure."

Three hours later, after X-rays, an MRI and lab work, the E.R. staff trundled Garrett out of emergency in a wheelchair and helped him up into the backseat of Ryan's truck.

"The doctor did want you to stay overnight," said one of the older nurses. "You can still change your mind."

At Garrett's vehement *no,* she reluctantly held out his discharge documents.

Kristin reached around Garrett to accept them. "We'll stay with him tonight, promise."

"Any problems, and he'll be in San Antonio, pronto," Ryan added. "Thanks for everything."

Garrett waited until they were out of the parking lot, then groaned. "No matter what that nurse said, no more docs. I'll be f-fine."

"Yeah, wait until those painkillers wear off and tell me that again." Ryan's sharp tone echoed the concern etched on his face as he glanced in the rearview mirror. "Maybe next time, you'll take better care of yourself."

Kristin twisted in her seat to look back at Garrett. The crimson hematoma covering his right cheek would be purple by morning; his eye was already swollen shut.

Two thousand pounds of angry bull had also given him three cracked ribs, a mild concussion and a killer headache. It was an absolute miracle he wasn't lying on a surgery table…or worse. "Are you comfortable enough back there?"

"Dandy," he snarled without opening his eyes. He grabbed at the Navajo saddle blanket draped across the backrest of his seat, then shifted so he could lean into the corner and draped the blanket over his long legs. "I still think you coulda called someone at the ranch and gotten the chopper over here."

"Trevor's gone for the weekend. Dad can't pilot any longer. Who's gonna bring it, Adelfa?"

Grumbling, Garrett tipped his black hat down over his eyes. "Jus' wake me up when we're home."

Miles of empty Texas prairie rolled by, marked by an occasional intersection boasting a gas station, or a few shabby, deserted buildings that might once have been the seeds of a small town.

"I'm sorry about this evening," Ryan murmured as he turned off the two-lane blacktop and onto a cloverleaf entrance for I-10. He glanced at the digital clock set in the dash. "Here you have a weekend alone to get lots of things done at your place, and you'll be too tired to do anything but sleep. We won't get back until three."

"Don't worry about it. I enjoyed the rodeo a great deal until Garrett got hurt. I haven't done anything like this since I was a kid. My dad…" Belatedly remembering that her father was a touchy subject at the Four Aces, she faltered to a stop. The heavy weight of sadness and loss settled into her chest. "He was a good man, Ryan. I know he had his faults, but…"

Ryan took her hand, giving it a gentle squeeze. "I'm not convinced my father and Leland are right about him. A man is innocent until proven guilty in my book."

"But you're working in the ranch's office, right?" The warmth of his hand felt so reassuring that she felt a glimmer of hope. "You'd be able to tell what happened?"

"It's not that easy. Nothing was computerized—or at least, not very well. A lot of documents are misfiled or incomplete, and while I'm trying to go through all of that, most of my time has to be spent on current business."

And he planned to leave in just two more months, leaving behind the Gallaghers who were already convinced of her father's crime. Her hope faded. "So in the end, my dad will take the blame and my son will always believe his grandfather was a thief."

"Whatever happened, you and your son had nothing to do with it."

Garrett stirred. She turned to look at him, then unbuckled her seat belt and reached back to lay her hand against his forehead. "How're you doing?"

He cracked open his good eye. "Like I can't wait to get out of this truck. Where are we, anyway?"

"Another hour." Ryan glowered at him in the rearview mirror. "Just be thankful we were there, or you'd be on a Greyhound—if there were any routes even close to that town—or you'd be hitching a ride back."

Kristin settled into her seat and fastened her seat belt. "He's still got an hour before he's due for another pain capsule."

"Anyone who wants to ride bulls for a living must be pretty tough. He'll live."

Ryan's words were harsh, but his profile, illuminated by the dim lights on the dashboard, revealed a much deeper concern for his brother than he wanted to show, Kristin decided. "I'm sure he will."

At the exit for Homestead, Ryan took the cloverleaf and headed into the darkness. Here and there, security lights glowed like distant stars on the hillsides, marking the otherwise invisible presence of ranches and acreages. He took a back road around the town itself, and a few miles later he turned up the drive to Cedar Grove Farm.

Kristin, who'd been checking on Garrett again, turned to Ryan in surprise. "Wait a minute—I said I'd come to the ranch with you. I can be there if he has any problems."

Ryan drove up to her front door before pulling

to a stop. Turning toward her, one wrist resting on the top of the steering wheel, he reached out and gently cupped her chin. "You've been wonderful. Three hours in an E.R. and having the privilege of listening to my ungrateful brother is more than anyone could ask."

"But—"

"I'll check on him every hour. He seems to be doing just fine, but if anything comes up I promise I'll call. Fair enough?"

He was so close, in the intimate confines of the cab, his light blue eyes shadowed by the thick crescents of his eyelashes, the lean angles of his face mysterious and compelling in the darkness. She imagined the feel of his kiss....

"Hey, man," Garrett mumbled drunkenly from the backseat. "I...I'm about...to barf. Get me... out..."

Ryan jerked back and flung open his door. In a heartbeat he had his arm around Garrett's shoulders. "C'mon, buddy. I've got you. Just nice, slow breaths, now..." Garret winced and cried out as Ryan eased him to his feet. "Any better?"

"Maybe the fresh air will help." Kristin moved to Garrett's other side. "This could be due to his mild concussion or the pain meds. Has he ever had any problem with codeine?"

Ryan looked blankly at her, but Garrett mumbled something that sounded like "yes."

"Apparently he has." Ryan took a half step back. "You could have said something when that nurse was taking your health history."

"What…nurse?" Garrett raised his head briefly and gave him a loopy grin. "Pretty?"

Ryan snorted in disgust. "Let's just get you home and into your own bed. The sooner the better."

But while Garrett had come out of the truck without much trouble, he now seemed to have pretty strong ideas about getting back in. Bracing an arm against the door frame, he dug in his heels. "Gonna be sick. Can't."

"Just fifteen, twenty minutes till we're home," Ryan said soothingly. "You made it this far, and this poor woman has had more than enough of both of us, I'm sure. Just get in. *Please.*"

Garrett gave Kristin a woozy, pleading smile. "I'd rather…walk."

"Look, it's no problem," Kristin said briskly. "You can leave him here on my couch—he won't have anything more than a few porch steps to navigate, and he'll be close to the bathroom. It could take a few more hours for the codeine to wear off, and that will be morning anyway."

Garrett pulled away from Ryan's grasp, braced his arms gingerly over his damaged ribs and turned awkwardly away to vomit in the bushes next to the truck.

"*Definitely,* leave him here," she added.

"Then I guess you'll have us both, because I can hardly leave you to deal with him alone." With a resigned sigh, Ryan reached into the truck for the ignition keys. "And if he starts feeling better, I can just haul him home. I'm sorry about all of this, Kristin."

Over the past few weeks, Kristin's thoughts had often wandered to the past.

She'd imagined Ryan's kiss, his touch…what it might be like to wrap her arms around him again. But never once had she dreamed that he might end up on her doorstep with his obstinate brother… and not want to be there at all.

CHAPTER FIFTEEN

GARRETT STARTED SNORING within minutes of hitting the couch in Kristin's living room.

After starting a fire in the fireplace, Ryan dusted off his hands and went over to check on him. "If he didn't weigh so much, I'd haul him out to the truck and take him home," he muttered. "He looks like he's well enough to travel."

"Maybe, but he sure wasn't faking how he felt an hour ago. That pain med is powerful stuff, so I'm sure he feels groggy. And every breath has to hurt, with those cracked ribs." She winced. "Just think how much it hurt when he lost his cookies outside."

"Maybe this will be a good lesson. Did you hear the nurse talking to him about his sprained wrist?" Ryan shook his head as he paced the darkened room. "He's had it since the last rodeo. Never had it looked at, didn't wrap it well, so all along he's been making it worse saddling and riding colts at the ranch. And that's his rope hand when he rides bulls, yet he still went out there and rode.

Just imagine the force and the torque on those weakened tendons. What was he thinking?"

"About all the fame and glory, I suppose. Maybe about proving himself to people he admires very much."

Ryan braced a hand on the mantel and stared into the flickering flames. "With his attitude, I can't imagine who that would be."

"You, your father. Trevor." Kristin perched on the arm of one of the upholstered chairs flanking the fireplace. "Just think about it. Your father is a powerful man—not just around here, but statewide. How can Garrett compete with that? Trevor is like Clint's right hand, and has a beautiful family. And you?" She smiled. "That's like trying to best a superman *and* James Bond."

The flames cast deep shadows on Ryan's face, emphasizing the lines of exhaustion bracketing his mouth. "Then Garrett is a lot more foolish than I thought."

"What, because he admires a brother who travels the world and has made a career of danger? I'll bet Garrett has envied you all these years, imagining excitement and death-defying missions. What younger brother wouldn't?"

"I've *never* told him about what I do." Ryan bowed his head, his eyes closed. "He wouldn't be so proud."

"Then maybe," she said gently, "it's time to

talk to him. I've heard about you around town, you know. You may not keep in touch with these people, but they all view you as a great hero."

"Well, I'm not," he said harshly. "I follow orders. I protect my men and I get the job done. But going through hell and back doesn't make me a hero. Not when—"

He broke off suddenly and paced the floor, his eyes bleak.

"You've been through a lot. The scars, what happened to your shoulder and knee—I can't even imagine the pain."

"It's no more than I…" His voice trailed off as he pulled to a stop in front of the windows and stared out into the night.

"Than what? Than you *deserve?*"

She watched him for a moment, then rose and wrapped her arms around his waist. She rested her cheek against his back. "I know what kind of man you are, Ryan. I remember who you were in college, and that hasn't changed in all these years. Whatever happened, I know it wasn't your fault… and that you couldn't have done more." She took a deep breath. "I also know that it helps to talk."

"Does it? Or does it just make everything more real? You have no idea. No idea at all." He stepped out of her embrace and moved into one of the chairs by the fireplace. Propping an elbow on the arm, he rested his head against his palm, staring into the flames.

Well, that hadn't gone as she'd hoped.

"Would you like some coffee? I have decaf. Or…" Kristin felt suddenly awkward and unsure. "If you want to catch a couple hours of sleep, you're welcome to Cody's room upstairs. I'm a little too wired right now to sleep anyway, so I can stay down here with Garrett."

"No. He's my responsibility."

"Maybe so, but sometimes responsibility can be shared, Ryan—like now." Kristin settled into the chair opposite his. "I get the feeling that you consider yourself responsible for way too much. Maybe you need to forget some of the things you just can't change."

"Nice try, Cantrell, but you tell me." He met her gaze with a weary one of his own. "If your actions meant a dozen children were badly injured or died—just how easy would it be to let that go?"

HE WAS THERE AGAIN.

Mortar fire shook the earth, raining pulverized concrete into the narrow street. Heavy clouds of pale gray dust obliterated everything but the rubble a few feet ahead of him and the faces of the locals running past him in fear of their lives.

Mothers held their small children, clutched tightly in their arms. Old men hobbled awkwardly, a thousand years of turmoil etched on their deeply lined faces.

Corporal Dietrich yelled something from a point just a few yards ahead, his voice lost in the constant staccato of automatic rifle fire.

A frightened young woman came running at him with terrified children at her heels—one with a bandaged head, some with crutches. Ryan stepped aside to let them pass, hoping against hope that they would all get out.

He ran for the building ahead, shouting for Dietrich and the others to follow him inside—his lungs burning, his mouth filled with the choking dust. The others hung back but he kept running. *There's still time…still time…*

Only later, days later, was he conscious enough to hear that he'd been too late.

The insurgents had made no empty threats before, and they'd not made one then, in their demand for the release of two of their leaders.

Four well-placed IEDs had detonated at the corners of the children's hospital. A suicide bomber hit the front doors a split second later…and no one even knew how many of the children died.

A section of wall had fallen on Ryan as he ran inside, crushing his knee and shoulder and knocking him unconscious, but it had also protected him from the explosive force of the jagged glass and metal fragments that landed a hundred yards away.

Maybe he'd been lucky to survive, but he hadn't deserved it.

"*Ryan*. Ryan…wake up. It's okay, it's okay."

He struggled to climb from the depths of the nightmare, even as warm, soft hands cradled his face. Soothing. Loving.

He opened his eyes and found Kristin kneeling in front of him, her eyes filled with tears.

"I'm so sorry," she whispered. "So very, very sorry. You were dreaming, I think. I heard you cry out for someone."

"It's nothing." He needed distance and would've stood and moved away, but the touch of her hands held him more securely than any shackles could have.

She rocked back on her heels and took his hands in hers. "That isn't true, Ryan. I understand that you don't want to talk about it—maybe you *can't*. But if there's anything I can do…"

He looked into her eyes and found such complete acceptance, such understanding, that something inside him cracked just a little…the wall of sorrow and guilt that he'd built so long ago. The anger at himself for failing.

Her hands still on his, he reached up to frame her lovely face and leaned closer to rest his forehead against hers.

There were no words.

There was no way to tell her…or to explain that he'd welcomed his multiple surgeries and long rehabilitation. The pain had felt like penance for the death of those nameless, faceless children. Because he'd been too late.

Kristin's hands trembled. "Let me…please…"

Then she leaned into him and kissed him.

There were a hundred reasons why this was wrong. A hundred reasons why both of them would regret this later.

Yet he kissed her back…and with that simple touch of his lips against hers, he felt as if he'd stepped into the past.

"ADELFA TELLS ME you and Garrett were off at some rodeo last night," Leland said. He raised an eyebrow. "You look beat, and I haven't even seen your brother around yet this morning. How'd it go?"

The Four Aces lawyer had arrived just as Ryan walked into the office at ten o'clock. He'd made small talk for the past half hour, keeping Ryan from tackling the hunting lease advertisements that needed to be emailed to the Dallas and Austin newspapers by noon, but the genial old guy was hard to ignore.

Perhaps for the best, because since Ryan had brought Garrett home, the only thing on his mind had been Kristin. Kissing her last night had been a mistake.

He'd spent too many years angry after they broke up and, even after the hurt had faded, he'd thought about her so often. At the oddest moments, he'd see her smile, hear her laughter. Remember all that had been between them.

He didn't want to hurt her. Didn't want to lead her on…and he also didn't want to face the coming years with her memory fresh in his mind.

Leland chuckled. "You look like you're a thousand miles away. How's your brother?"

"He took a fall in the chute with the bull on top of him."

"Is he hurt?"

"No casts, no stitches, but he's going to be feeling that fall for a long time. Hold on just a minute." Ryan proofread a hard copy of the ad, turned to the computer to make some minor changes and printed off a final copy. He emailed it off before turning back to Leland. "Dad isn't here, if you were looking for him. He's in Austin."

Leland shrugged. "Guess I should've called, but this is my day to be in the Homestead office, and Clint is usually around. How are things going?"

"It's all just as complex as you'd said it would be. I'm making some headway, though. The computer I ordered arrived last week, along with updated business software, so bringing this place into the twenty-first century and keeping up with the bills takes most of my time."

"And the older books? Seen any sign of that missing money?"

"There hasn't been much time, yet. This place is like the Aegean stable of mythology. As fast as I work, there's more coming in."

Leland nodded in sympathy. "We did make it through taxes the past couple years, and the ranch hasn't been audited so far. Maybe you're better off moving ahead, for now."

"That's your legal opinion?" Ryan frowned. "Given the fines and interest that could accrue?"

"It's not ideal, but just getting this business organized and back on its feet will be an accomplishment. An awful lot was left undone over the past few years."

Ryan studied him. "You're probably right."

"Have you found anything suspicious—any evidence Nate left behind?" Lines creased Leland's brow. "I expected a cowboy like him would leave a paper trail a mile wide, but he was one crafty dude."

"Must've been," Ryan said mildly.

Leland lingered for a while, discussing investments and accounts, then clapped Ryan affectionately on the back. "I'd better get to town. Tell your dad I stopped by."

Ryan watched him drive away before turning to

the computer. But until he finally closed down the current month's file in the accounting program, he couldn't shake one thought.

Were there secrets somewhere in all of those old invoices? Could there be a clear trail leading to the true culprit?

Everyone was convinced Nate had embezzled all the money, but the errors hadn't started with him.

Ryan had gone through some of the oldest files, and had come up with one error after another. Carefully altered records. Invoices that didn't match the cancelled checks.

And all of them were dated before Nate was hired.

AFTER RYAN AND GARRETT left at dawn, Kristin spent the rest of the morning trying to avoid dwelling on the night before. *You're pathetic,* she muttered to herself as she scrubbed the kitchen floor by hand, then flew into a frenzy dusting every nook and cranny. *Pathetic, pathetic, pathetic.*

She could only imagine what Ryan thought of her now, after she'd practically kissed him the moment he walked in her door. She'd wanted to give him comfort, healing. She'd wanted to...

With a snort, she headed for the upstairs bedrooms. She hadn't just wanted to give him emotional support. She'd wanted to kiss him. But she'd felt herself almost in tears—it was all such a vivid reminder of everything she'd lost when they'd broken up.

Her life had gone on, and so had his. But if she could do one thing over, she'd go back and fight harder to keep him. Clint had been a terrifying, powerful figure to her as a shy young college girl. His threats had rung true. But with her adult perspective, she realized that she and Ryan could have stood up to him, found a way to be together.

But second chances didn't come along often, and she already knew that this chance intersection of her life with Ryan was a very temporary thing.

In Cody's room she dusted and picked up, then sank onto his bed and stared at the collection of books and toys and sports equipment jammed onto the built-in shelves. Loneliness snuck up on her as she absorbed the silence of the old house.

It wouldn't be long until Cody reached middle school, then high school and, after that, the years without him at home seemed to stretch on forever. What would it be like, being totally alone? Nothing she looked forward to, unlike some of her friends back in Dallas.

With a sigh, she picked up her dust cloth and started for the door, passing the small framed photo of her father on Cody's desk.

Her frustration welled again at the dead end

she'd reached with Buddy's Auto Shop. She'd been so sure she'd find the old truck. *Right.* Sitting there, waiting for her after nearly two years. What had she been thinking?

Any evidence would be long gone.

Ryan wouldn't be in town long enough to prove anything even if he *did* want to. Besides, after last night, he'd probably be putting as much distance as possible between himself and the Cantrells.

So this whole town would go on, convinced Nate had been a lowlife, an embezzler who'd stolen from his boss.

Yet all she'd needed was to find some sort of proof. A scrape, maybe, and some paint residue on Dad's truck. Surely there'd have been *something* if another person had driven him off the road. Just last month, someone had opened a door against the side of her truck in a parking lot, and even that light touch had left a long green mark from the other car's paint.

She brushed a fingertip against her father's photograph. "I'm sorry, Dad...I guess we'll never know."

Her gaze dropped to the collection of Hot Wheels cars arranged on the desk. Cody played with them for hours upon hours, staging races and crashes, sometimes sending them catapulting down the stairs. Idly, she rested a finger on one and scooted it back and forth, then bumped it against the side of another car.

She stared at them for a moment, then did it again.

The sheriff's photos had included a shot of the truck's course down the hill. It had gone down nose first, then apparently ricocheted off a large boulder and begun a sideways, bouncing rollover to the bottom of the ravine.

She'd figured that someone might have sideswiped the truck, and that there could've been paint residue on the doors.

But what if another driver had rammed just the front fender...or had cut sharply into the path of the truck? Could there have been any contact with the corner of Dad's *bumper*?

The piles of auto parts stacked behind Buddy's Auto... It was a long shot. Probably just another dead end, another disappointment. But if she didn't at least try, she would never know.

CHAPTER SIXTEEN

KRISTIN MADE IT to Buddy's Auto by three minutes after noon. This time, she ignored the Closed sign and rapped sharply on the door, then skirted the shop and went around back calling his name.

Sure enough, he soon stepped out of an open garage door leading into the building, wiping his hands on a greasy rag. "Hey," he called out in greeting.

She picked her way through the pieces of machinery lying everywhere. "Hey."

He cocked his head. "Lookin' for ole trucks again, or are you just takin' a tour?"

"Pieces this time, actually." She surveyed the jumble of automotive parts stacked in piles or leaning against a long corrugated metal shed. "If you have an old vehicle...not worth much...you part it out, right?"

"Probably."

"Bumpers or front fenders?"

"Depends, I guess...." His voice trailed off as he surveyed his stock, then glanced up the hill at the junk graveyard, where rows of old trucks, old tractors and cars were parked. "You know your daddy's truck is long gone."

"I'm just hoping you might've taken off anything usable before having it crushed."

"Maybe." He rubbed his chin. "Those '67 Chevys were real popular, but it ain't always easy to find original parts. Sometimes we'll even save parts with a little damage, if we figure a body man can fix 'em."

"And don't you have some sort of system, a way to know what you've got—by year and model?"

He released a gusty sigh. "Yes, ma'am. But that don't mean it's in some fancy computer. You saw my book last time."

Complete with grease stains and half-legible writing, but she'd also seen meticulous detail. "The car parts out here, do they all have some sort of stock number on them? A way for you to keep your inventory straight?"

He hooted at that. "Mighty good idea, if I had a half-dozen guys working here, round-the-clock." His expression grew somber. "I do miss your daddy, and I'm real sorry for your loss. Look, I'll search around a little. If I parted out that old '67 Chevy, I might have chalked the invoice numbers underneath the bigger pieces. That's the best I can do. Got a phone number?"

Kristin dug into her purse and handed him a business card from the clinic. "I'd be happy to help look. I've seen photos and I know it was gray with white or cream fenders and a shiny silver front bumper."

"Right." He tipped his head toward the sea of metal behind him. "That will help a lot—but I don't want no one else back here. My insurance man is pretty doggone firm about that."

"But you will check?"

He pocketed her card in the front center pocket of his overalls. "I'll check, but don't be holding your breath. This is a real shot in the dark."

"Thank you." She hesitated, then stood on her toes to give him a peck on the cheek. "Thank you *so* much."

"WE'VE GOTTEN THREE MORE calls on hunting leases, Dad." Ryan opened a file on the desk and flipped through it. "Two guys from Dallas and one from San Antonio. I figure there's enough prime hunting land here for you to set up another seven or eight leases."

"Tried that ten years ago. Not worth the bother," Clint said dismissively. "Fools left gates open. Left their trash. Lost two good steers when one idiot didn't take aim."

"It's worth the trouble now. Hunting is huge in Texas, as you well know. Something like ninety-seven percent of the land is privately owned, so you've got to get in there, Dad. Wealthy hunters are willing to pay top dollar to use your land."

Clint waved impatiently. "Trevor's too busy. You'll soon be gone. Who do you think is going to manage all of this?"

"Garrett and Trevor. The person you hire to replace me." Ryan slid a copy of a new ad layout across the table. "We can designate certain areas for three-day hunting party packages at $395 to $500 per gun, and offer the use of some cabins that are empty anyway. Annual leases in other areas of the ranch ought to go for around $2,500 per gun."

"And what makes you think that?"

"Since Trevor got back from Houston, he's spent the last four days doing flyovers with the chopper, checking for game. This ranch hasn't been hunted much in years, and he's counted hundreds of whitetail and uncountable flocks of turkeys, and that's just what he can see from the air. Ride any direction from the barns and you'll find flocks of quail and dove. Hunters will bag their limits and beg to come back."

Clint pursed his lips as he scanned the advertisement Ryan had created on the computer. "You can get this show on the road before you leave?"

"We'll likely be turning people away. Leland is working on several standard contracts specifying dates, liability and so on. Then it'll just be a matter of fielding calls and answering questions."

"Leland tells me he talked to you last weekend, by the way." Clint drummed his fingers on the desk.

"He came to the office, looking for you. He thinks Nate was 'one crafty dude' to figure out such a slick embezzlement scheme…and he figures that you'll never track down the money."

"I was a fool. A trusting fool."

"Well, I don't think the problem started with Nate. He *may* have taken the opportunity to continue siphoning, but I've found problems that predate his employment."

Clint glowered at him. "Minor errors. Sloppy bookkeeping."

"Not just that. If you want to know the truth, I'm beginning to doubt Nate was guilty. I think someone else has been cooking the books for a long time. Oscar had the most access to the records…or it could've been an assistant foreman. I understand there've been several coming and going over the past ten years."

"I had an expert in here—an accountant who knew what he was doing," Clint snapped. "That isn't what he found. Leland is like a brother to me, and he concurred. Then you waltz in here after all these years and think you know it all. What could you possibly know about this ranch? The people here?"

"Maybe that accountant just didn't have the time to dig deep enough." Ryan shrugged. "Either way, the money's long gone, but I'm going to get to the bottom of it before I leave. I think it's only fair to find the truth."

"It's that Cantrell woman, isn't it?" Clint said flatly. "You think you're gonna find some way to clear her father's name and be a big hero." Clint glared at him as he abruptly rose to his feet. "You can twist the facts however you like, but that doesn't change a thing. Hiring Nate was the biggest mistake of my life, and you're a fool if you think you can prove otherwise."

Ryan looked right back at him, not giving an inch. "I'm not the enemy here, Dad. I'm on *your* side, remember?"

"My side?" Clint laughed harshly. "Your brothers were good sons. They stayed here, and made something of themselves, rather than running off like a fool to some other part of the world just to prove a point."

Ryan tactfully resisted the temptation to mention Garrett's vagabond rodeo career. "I joined the *service,* Dad, not a circus. Serving my country has been an honorable career."

"One you wouldn't have chosen if you hadn't been so hell-bent on defying me. And what happened? You nearly got yourself killed." Clint cursed under his breath and stormed out of the office.

Bemused, Ryan watched him leave. But when he got back to work, Clint's words kept playing through his mind.

There'd never been much love lost between them. Ryan had stood up to Clint's domination even as a small boy. But just now there'd been something besides anger in his father's voice. *Worry.*

And that, Ryan figured, was as close as he was ever going to get to an expression of love from his father.

AT NINE TWENTY-SEVEN on Sunday morning, Clint marched up the steps of St. Mark's Episcopal Church as he did each week, nodding to the local ranchers and townsfolk he'd seen there for the past fifty years.

He ignored the new faces in the crowd until he reached the Gallagher pew, second row from the front, right side—and found a family of squabbling children and a very pregnant woman filling the entire space. *His* pew.

His jaw working, he glowered at them.

There was plenty of room elsewhere, but she was too ignorant to take a hint.

Another family of homesteaders, no doubt.

Freeloaders who'd come to grab good land and waste every precious resource on it.

The woman smiled back, oblivious to her mistake and the sudden hush that swept through the half-empty church. "We can just slide in," she stage-whispered. "There's room."

As if.

Conscious of the openmouthed stares of those at the back of the church, Clint moved stiffly to the next pew up and sat with his arms folded and jaw set.

A dwindling congregation had led to fading resources, and when there'd been decisions to make, he'd put himself front and center on every score. Gallagher money had kept this church going for the past twenty years. He deserved respect.

During the sermon, he stared up at silver-haired Father Holden, who stood at the pulpit delivering a strong sermon on tithing, and decided that he and the big-boned Irishman needed to have a talk in the near future.

Holden's wife, Ruth, was on that meddling Home Free committee along with Enfield and several others. They were upsetting the balance of how things had always been, and the audacious woman sitting behind him, with a litter of unkempt kids and no husband in sight, was a case in point.

Soon there'd be even more people on the welfare rolls in Loveless County, and all because of a misguided group who had nothing better to do than stir up trouble. It was definitely time to make his displeasure known.

Holden had been admonishing the congregation about grateful giving for a full ten minutes when Clint felt someone touch his shoulder. *One of the rug rats in the pew behind him, no doubt.* He scowled irritably and jerked away, but at the second, persistent touch he glanced over to find Lydia easing into the pew next to him.

Lydia.

They'd kept careful distance from one another since their divorce—their mutual animosity as effective as a high-voltage electric fence—and she'd once sworn she would never again set foot in this church.

Beneath the brim of her lacy beige hat, her skin appeared sallow, her cheekbones sharply defined in her thin face. Her hand felt bony on his arm. "Forgive me. I didn't mean to interrupt."

He held himself rigid and didn't spare her a glance for the rest of the service. But his dread grew, and he found himself wishing Holden would double the length of his sermon.

Because he really didn't want to hear what Lydia had to say.

FOR OVER A WEEK, Kristin called Buddy daily, asking if he'd found anything that could have been a part on her father's truck.

On Monday morning, he left a message for her at the clinic while she was busy with a physical, and by noon she was nearly biting her nails in anticipation.

"Wish me luck," she called out to Max as she grabbed her purse, reached inside for her keys and started for the door. "I should be back in forty-five minutes. Call my cell if you need me."

"Uh…before you leave…" Max hiked a thumb toward the waiting room. "There's someone else here to see you."

Kristin sighed. Buddy had promised to meet her at twelve, but then he was going out of town for two weeks. She couldn't stand the prospect of waiting that much longer. "A drop-in?"

"Of sorts." He winked at her. "Better go check him out."

In his lab coat embroidered with romping kittens Max really was the most adorable man. Despite his burly frame and all those tattoos, he'd proven to be a gentle soul…rather like a congenial grandpa who just happened to be a bodybuilder on the side.

Rolling her eyes, she dropped her purse on the counter in the lab on her way back down the hall.

"I don't have much time," she whispered as she passed him.

But even before she reached the waiting room she felt a shivery awareness. And sure enough, she found Ryan, his Stetson at his side.

During the past week he'd invited Cody over after school every day, so her son had taken the school bus home with Hayden, and the three of them had spent an hour or so practicing football passes. She'd come for Cody as soon as she finished at the clinic.

She and Ryan had been cordial. Even friendly. But neither one of them had mentioned the night of the rodeo or the fact that they'd stepped over an invisible line with that kiss.

He probably thought it had been a mistake, and she was still embarrassed because she'd so carelessly let her feelings show. With his family's name and wealth, he'd probably had to fend off his share of golddiggers. Did he think she was just another woman with dollar signs in her eyes?

"I need to talk to you, without the little cowboys underfoot. I hoped you might have some time over lunch," he said, a corner of his mouth lifting in a faint grin. "I'll buy."

She shot a swift glance at her watch. "I...can't. I'm sorry."

"Max told me you were just leaving. If you have other plans..."

"An errand. But it can't wait."

"I know things have been a little…awkward, this past week or so. You come by to pick up Cody, and then you're gone in a flash." Lowering his voice, he regarded her with troubled eyes. "I want to apologize for what happened after the rodeo. You were just being…kind, and I took things too far."

She looked away and felt warmth rise into her face. "I…um…figured it was my fault."

"Fault implies something was wrong, Kris. And I…" His gaze veered toward the receptionist's desk. "Maybe I'd better come by another time. I also need to talk about your father."

She glanced over her shoulder at Max, who was now working on medical insurance forms, and swiftly debated what to do. "Look, I need to get to Buddy's within the next half hour. I could meet you at the café for lunch afterward, if you'd like."

"Or I could just tag along." He grinned and jingled his truck keys. "Four Aces Chauffeur, at your service."

He was a Gallagher. One of the enemy camp, and his dad might've had something to do with her father's death, for all she knew. But she'd also heard Ryan express doubt about Nate's guilt and his determination to uncover the truth.

Maybe Ryan hadn't fought hard enough to keep her years ago, but she'd never doubted his integrity or absolute conviction about doing the right thing.

"All right, then. It might be easier to talk in your truck instead of the café, anyway."

BUDDY MET THEM in front of his shop. He gave her a quizzical look when he saw Ryan, but she just shrugged.

"I think you'll be interested in this," he said. "Come on around back and take a look."

She followed him through the rubble, cautiously sidestepping sharp bits of metal protruding from the various heaps of junked parts.

Ryan followed close behind, with his hand at her elbow. "You need something for your truck?"

"Not exactly." She debated how much to say. "I'm...looking for something that belonged to my dad."

They followed as Buddy ambled to the end of the long metal shed, then over a grassy patch to the door of another, much smaller building. "Careful, ma'am—I got a rattler out here. A five-footer, easy."

She shuddered, scanning the ground before carefully making her way to his side. "They've got plenty of places to hide around here."

"And since I almost never come out here, there's probably nests of 'em everywhere." Buddy jangled through a ring of keys suspended from his belt, trying several in the padlock, until one finally worked. The door swung open with a rusty squeal, and he reached inside to flip on a light switch. "Couple years ago, I had an employee help me do some organizing. Big mistake, 'cause I never did figure out his system and then he moved on. God only knows what's in here—or in some of the other sheds."

She tried to hide her growing disappointment. "So you haven't actually been back here to check?"

Buddy chuckled. "Scared a lot of rats and a coupla black widows, so I didn't linger. But with you calling about them parts every day, I finally figured the varmints would be easier to deal with. I think I have what you want."

From the way he stepped cautiously across the floor, he wasn't kidding about the varmints. Suppressing a shudder, she followed him, thankful for Ryan's reassuring presence at her side.

Buddy grabbed a long piece of metal pipe off the floor and tentatively poked at some crumbling cardboard boxes, then kicked them aside.

Stacked against the wall was a collection of car and truck fenders. At least half a dozen of them, in assorted models and colors.

"I didn't go through all of them, but I did see a pair of '67 Chevy front fenders out here last night. Thing is, I think Ralph must've smudged my chalk numbers when he was moving things around. And the fenders don't match."

Kristin took a sharp breath. "What color?"

"Sorta tan and a black."

Her excitement kicked up another notch. "Both for a '67?"

"Yes, ma'am. They're a little rusty on the edges, but Ralph must have stripped them off anyway." Buddy shifted several fenders, then hauled out the two he'd mentioned.

"So you aren't hunting down parts for your own truck, then," Ryan said quietly. "This would be something from your dad's truck."

"My Aunt Nora is *convinced* he was forced off the road."

They stepped over to where Buddy had laid out the two fenders. The beige one was pockmarked with gravel dings, but had no suspicious scrapes or marks.

The black one—driver's side—bore more significant rust along the bottom, a patch of primer and a deep horizontal crease. But instead of any telltale paint residue, the crease had rusted to a dusty orange.

She couldn't contain her disappointment. "I...I'd hoped..."

"It still might be possible for a lab to find what you need." Ryan squeezed her shoulder. "Though that scrape could've come at any time. Even years before your dad's accident."

Kristin pulled out her wallet. "How much for the black one?"

Buddy scratched his head and looked at her. "I don't think this is gonna help none. You don't know for sure if this is even the right one."

"I can compare it to the sheriff's photos," she said firmly. She started counting out bills from the meager collection in her wallet, then pulled out her Visa. "What's something like this worth?"

He held up his hands, palms out. "Take it. Keep it long as you need it, if you think it will be any help. Like I said before, Nate was a good friend. It's the least I can do."

CHAPTER SEVENTEEN

AFTER A CALL to Max, Kristin agreed to stop for a quick lunch at Bertha's Kolaches, a small lunch-room on the town square and just a half block away from the clinic. One of the few places in the area with decent food, Bertha's offered sandwiches and soups in addition to its namesake pastries.

Ryan guided Kristin past the old-fashioned lunch counter to one of the few small tables in the back. "I used to come here after high school with my buddies," he said, glancing at the old-style pressed-tin ceiling and vinyl upholstered stools fixed along the counter. "I don't think a single thing has changed—except the prices."

"I vaguely remember being here, too, when I was little." After a middle-aged waitress took their orders and brought them coffee, she surreptitiously glanced at her watch. She hoped there'd still be enough time to make it to the sheriff's office with the truck fender. "I wish I remembered seeing you here."

"You left town years before I was old enough

to drive, so that wasn't likely. My dad wasn't one for idle visits to town or for wasting time when we did get in. He mostly left us at home. Other than school and church, we were rarely off the ranch."

"How is Garrett doing, by the way?"

"Better. His ribs are still sore and he's been lying around all week, having Adelfa wait on him. Our mother showed up again yesterday, so she's fussing over him, too."

"How about his concussion? Is he still having headaches?"

"With Garrett, I suspect everything is always a little worse than it really is. He seems to be doing fine until he knows someone is coming."

Garrett must've been a young boy when his mother walked out, so that wasn't surprising. "He probably soaks up the attention, don't you think?"

"That he does. I did find out why he was so sick on the way home, though, and why he refused to get back into the truck at your place."

"Not the codeine?"

"Adelfa says he gets carsick, and can't handle being in a backseat at all. *Ever.*" A hint of amusement sparkled in Ryan's eyes. "He was sure embarrassed when she told me. It doesn't do much for his rough, tough bull rider image."

"How on earth does he handle those spinning bulls? Poor guy." Kristin sipped at her mug of steaming coffee. "I suppose the pain meds from the E.R. made him woozy enough that he just got in the backseat of your truck without a second thought."

The waitress brought their sandwiches and chips, then bustled away to take care of the only other customers, who'd just taken seats at the lunch counter near the window.

Despite their relative privacy, Ryan lowered his voice. "Lucky break on that fender."

Kristin swallowed a bite of her egg salad on rye. "If it's the right one—and if it even has any evidence on it. This is my one and only lead. The sheriff wasn't very encouraging, so I hope he'll follow through."

"My father is still convinced that Nate was responsible for the losses at the ranch, but I'm not. I want you to know that I'll keep working on it until I figure it out." He hesitated. "How close were you to your dad?"

"I didn't see him as often as I wanted to. Mom and I lived over three hundred miles away, and she and Dad didn't have an amicable divorce. He worked endless hours on one ranch or another, but saw me when he could."

"So he could have had, say, a gambling problem and you wouldn't have known."

"Gambling?" Kristin thought of the work-worn man with the weary eyes who'd struggled to provide support checks even after his ex-wife

had told him they weren't needed. "I wouldn't believe it. He wasn't a particularly social man. He wouldn't have been comfortable in a casino. He had a number of financial reverses, and I remember him being very frugal."

"He wouldn't need to be in a casino to gamble."

"Why—" Realization dawned, and she glared at Ryan. "I suppose you all think that's where the money went."

"It isn't my theory. I'm just asking."

Kristin glanced pointedly at her watch, then dug a ten-dollar bill out of her purse and dropped it on the table. "I need to get going or I won't make it to the sheriff's office in time."

He reached across the table and caught her hand. "I don't want us to argue over this, Kris. I *want* your father cleared. For your sake and for Cody's."

"If I'm defensive, I'm sorry." She sank back in her chair, his warm hand still on hers, his thumb rubbing circles gently against her wrist. "I...I'm not the girl I was back in college. Things haven't always been easy. I've had to fight for what I believe in. That won't change."

"I sure hope not." His gaze moved slowly over her face. "I know we've had a rocky start here, and maybe things moved too fast after the rodeo. I don't think either of us was ready to handle that just yet. But I'd like to see you again. A real date—not with the kids, not with my obstinate brother. Friday? Saturday?" He grinned boyishly. "Tomorrow?"

"I…" She thought about her resolution to keep her distance. The fact that the entire situation was just too complex right now. She had no business becoming involved with a Gallagher. Especially one who'd soon disappear into some war zone and possibly never return.

But that very fact made it impossible to say no. Whatever time she could have, she would take. No one else had ever held her heart so completely. And no one ever would.

"Yes," she whispered. "Friday…Saturday…and tomorrow sound just fine."

BY THE TIME THEY LEFT Bertha's, it was five minutes past one and Kristin had to hurry back to the clinic for a full schedule of patients.

Ryan helped her put the fender in the back of her truck, gave her a swift kiss, then headed back to the ranch, while she counted the minutes until five o'clock when she could go to see the sheriff.

She also spent an inordinate amount of time thinking about that kiss, and long afterward, she still felt the warmth of his touch.

During a brief lull—a no-show mom with two toddlers—she hurried down the block to the Snip and Curl, where she found RaeJean, dressed today in a pink uniform with a matching ruffled lace bow in her hair. She was taking payment for a permanent at the front desk.

As soon as the client left, her aunt's face lit up. "Well, bless your heart," RaeJean exclaimed. "It's so nice to see you! Do you have time to sit a spell?"

"Actually, I've just got a couple minutes between patients, and I've come to ask a favor." There were just two clients still in the shop and both were under hair dryers in the back, but Kristin lowered her voice anyway. "I need to find a babysitter for Cody. Next Saturday. Do you know of anyone? A client, maybe?"

RaeJean drew herself up, a frothy pink picture of indignation. "And what about his great-aunt?"

Kristin had been thinking more along the lines of a high school tomboy who could play catch or video games. "I just figured you must be tired, working such long days. I don't want to take advantage of you."

"Take advantage? My gracious, no. I'd be *thrilled.*" Her smile widened. "In fact, he could have a sleepover! We could rent some movies and bake cookies. I have a nice guest room, you know."

"Well..."

"It's all set, dear. Don't you worry your little head about a thing." RaeJean beamed at her. "This will be such fun—I never got to have children of my own, you know. I can't wait! Oh, and if you ever need me again, just say the word." A timer dinged on one of the hair dryers. "Oops, gotta run. You tell little Cody we'll have a good time."

Bemused, Kristin watched her aunt scurry back to the hair dryers. RaeJean truly had a heart of gold, but whether or not *little Cody* saw it that way could be an entirely different matter.

THANKFUL THAT CODY had gone home with Hayden after school again, Kristin called the sheriff's office, then parked near the door at a quarter after five. Wade came outside to meet her a few minutes later.

"So, you think you've found some evidence?" He rubbed his chin as she opened the cab-level camper shell on the back of her truck. "Where'd you get this?"

"Buddy's. The truck itself was crushed quite a while ago, but he did find some of the salvaged parts."

Wade frowned. "But how can you be sure this is the right fender?"

"You showed me photos—and Dad did have a black fender. This is the right make and year, and at least part of the number chalked on the underside matches the record on Dad's truck."

"Part of it?"

"Some are too blurry to read, but too many things match up for this to be a coincidence. And look at that area with primer—I bet we'll see it on those photos."

"Okay. So it could be the fender on your dad's truck. I'm still not sure that this will prove anything, ma'am."

She tried to rein in her frustration. "But look at this damage. It could've been made by someone veering into him as he was driving. If someone accidentally—or purposefully—crowded him, that might have sent him into the ravine."

"I had an investigator from San Antonio look over that truck, but he didn't come up with anything that could prove your theory." Wade pulled the fender out onto the tailgate of the truck and into the sunlight, and studied the long, narrow crease. "Maybe...just maybe, a lab could still pick up some paint residue in there, under the rust. But how could you prove exactly when this damage was done? It might have been six months earlier. A year. Since this fender didn't match the color of the truck, it could've occurred when it was on a different vehicle."

Remembering Clint's animosity toward her father and her, Kristin impulsively grabbed Wade's forearm. "*Please.* It's all I have to go on. If a lab can find out what make of vehicle caused this damage, maybe everything will fall into place."

Wade hesitated, obviously thinking she was being overly dramatic. "If I send this to the lab, you won't necessarily get a definitive answer. There could be hundreds of trucks of the same make, model and year in this county alone. And we can't prove this fender was hit here in Homestead, instead of Dallas or Timbuktu."

"I understand."

"We can't prove *when* it happened, either."

"I understand that, too."

"And this could take a good long while. This isn't going to be high priority for the lab."

She looked straight at him. "But maybe this *is* a homicide."

"Maybe," Wade said gently. "I'm just warning you that we won't be getting any answers back overnight." He studied the fender again. "Let's start by looking at those photos to make sure we have a match. If we do, then I'll send this in right away, and I'll push them for an answer as soon as possible. Deal?"

She nodded, waiting by her truck while he went in after the accident report. When he came out with the pictures in his hand, he was frowning.

"We took a lot of photos, especially of the damaged areas of the truck." He held one of them out, and glanced between the photo and the fender.

"You have the right one, for sure. And look here at this close-up."

He held out another photo that detailed the narrow horizontal crease—and revealed bare, gleaming metal. It wasn't rusted. Though it might've just been the camera flash reflecting off sharp facets in the metal, she thought she could see some flecks of green.

He pursed his lips and shook his head. "It was winter when this happened. Damp for this part of Texas. That could account for the rust coming on so soon. That truck probably sat out in the weather and the weeds for a good while before it was crushed.... And then maybe the fender just laid out there in Buddy's back lot for a spell, too. I figured the rust could have been from years past, but these pictures prove me wrong."

"So you believe me?"

"I believe it's worth a try. We still can't absolutely prove that your daddy wasn't dinged by another vehicle *before* his accident...but given his trajectory down that ravine, I'd guess you're right. If the lab can ferret out any foreign paint chips underneath that rust, at least we'll have a better idea."

"And you would follow up? There must be a database on vehicle models and colors."

"It isn't quite as easy as you see on those TV shows, ma'am, but I'll take this to the lab in

Austin at the end of the week." Wade hoisted the fender out of her truck. "And believe me, I'll do everything I can."

RIGHT AFTER CHURCH on Sunday, Clint's cell phone rang. He'd welcomed the call, and the excuse to take off for Austin overnight for a meeting with his campaign manager, as soon as Trevor could get the chopper ready. Lydia had leveled a look of bored nonchalance at him as he made his excuses and left, but he knew how well she could mask her true feelings.

Now that he was back home again, it was only a matter of time before she came after him. Even before he saw her pearl-gray Lincoln parked close to the house, he felt a sense of doom.

Steeling himself, he walked through the main entrance, dropped his suit bag at the door and continued to his office. An eerie sense of emptiness pervaded the house, though surely Adelfa and Lydia were here somewhere. Disgusted by his wayward thoughts, he sorted through the big stack of mail on his desk.

Squinting, he held the first letter close—then farther away. He flipped on the bright halogen desk lamp and adjusted his trifocals. The words swam together like a dizzying school of minnows, just beyond his ability to understand them. He finally slammed the document down and rubbed his eyes.

"So it's true."

The soft voice, which seemed to come out of nowhere, nearly made him jump out of his skin.

"It's me, Lydia. Over here."

He turned off the glaring desk lamp and saw her curled up in an overstuffed leather chair in the corner. Wearing some sort of flowing caftan of muted grays, even now she blended into the shadows.

"What are you doing in here?"

"Realizing that we're both getting old. Who would've guessed?"

"Happens," he shot back, irritated. "If that's all you had to say, leave me in peace."

"I will, darling. But not just yet."

Feeling a sudden chill, he reacted the only way he knew—with the anger that had marked their relationship for the past thirty years. "You think we have anything to say to each other? I can't imagine what." He shoved his chair back and launched to his feet. "If you feel a need to be here, then I'll leave."

"Sit, Clint. Don't make this any harder than it already is." He halted halfway out the door. "I don't have the energy to hunt you down, but you can bet I will."

He turned slowly and shut the door, then silently waited for the words he knew were coming.

"I didn't go to New York. I was having chemo in Dallas." She laughed. "It isn't the first time. Five years ago, and then two, thanks to my lovely cigarettes...and now it's spread. I'm not trying to fool myself about the future."

He didn't know what to say. She'd always been indomitable. A force as powerful as the never-ending Texas wind, with keen intelligence and a code of ethics that had brooked no excuses.... She'd bent to no one.

Until he'd threatened their children.

"I know this isn't going to break your heart, so don't even try to say something appropriate," she added with a dry laugh. "I'm sure the world will be a more peaceful place without the two of us in it."

And though they hadn't lived together for three decades and had fought throughout the decade before that, the world suddenly felt like a very *empty* place.

In all these years, he'd never imagined anyone or anything could get the better of his Lydia.

"When?" he managed, once he'd found his voice. "How long?"

"I haven't exactly made an appointment. The doc says three months, maybe four. But what does he know?"

It was so much easier being at war with her. He turned, helpless, needing to take some sort of action or provide a solution. But there was absolutely nothing he could do. Unless...

"What about doctors someplace else? Mayo? Out East?"

"I've checked every avenue. Somehow, I'd always thought I could accept death easily enough. But my values changed a tad when I was actually confronted with it." She gave an airy wave of her hand. "And now, I've decided I'd rather have quality time than a messy fight that makes my last months miserable."

"You'll stay here, then," he announced rather than asked, needing to take control of a situation that had veered too far from reality to comprehend. She only smiled back at him.

"Nothing will change. I've got my place in Dallas. I'll be back to visit the boys and my grandchildren, while I can. I don't," she added firmly, "want them to know."

"Is that *fair?*"

"I don't want them to know just yet," she amended. "I'll tell them in a couple months. Until then, I want good memories for them, not sad ones."

"You're wrong, Lydia."

"Am I? Take a hard look at what you stole from

me all those years ago. What you stole from the boys. And then tell me you don't owe us all this one good thing."

CHAPTER EIGHTEEN

ON TUESDAY NIGHT, Ryan took Kristin to dinner along the Riverwalk in San Antonio, then to a raucous, honky-tonk dance hall that might have come straight out of an old Western movie, where they laughed and danced until she was almost too dizzy and giddy to stand.

They made it back to Homestead at two in the morning, then curled up on her couch in front of the fireplace, slipping easily back into the old camaraderie they'd had in college.

Not until he'd regretfully glanced at his watch and stood up had he kissed her. Only caution and common sense had helped her step away, but an hour later, she still felt his touch.

On Friday night RaeJean happily babysat Cody again, this time with plans to take him out to Nora's ranch where they would have a cookout and a moonlight trail ride. Meanwhile Ryan took Kristin to a quiet little restaurant on the south side of Austin, where the jazz was smooth and the seafood superb.

This time, they lingered on her porch until very

late, listening to oldies on the radio and the coyotes howling up in the hills.

Ryan glanced at his wristwatch and then unfolded himself from the pile of pillows on the porch swing. He held out a hand to help Kristin up. "Guess I'd better head back," he said, his voice gravelly with the late hour and laced with regret. "I promised Trevor I'd help move cattle in the morning."

"It's morning already. You aren't going to get much sleep." Darkened with five o'clock shadow and cast in deep relief by the moonlight, his lean, hard face was so compelling she couldn't resist touching his cheek.

He caught her hand and held it, warmth in his eyes. "You're just as beautiful as you ever were, Kristin."

He'd be gone in less than two months. She'd already accepted that he wouldn't stay. But for now, she could build memories…memories that would have to last a lifetime, because no one would ever take his place in her heart.

"You're even more handsome now, if that's possible," she replied, feeling breathless.

"Thank you for a great night." He started to back away, but she kept hold of his hand. He let her pull him back toward her, and then bent down to kiss her. When she could take it no longer, she gently pushed him away.

"Go. You need sleep before you have to move those cows."

He grinned at her. "Sleep is overrated," he said as he made his way down her steps.

She watched him leave until she couldn't see his taillights anymore.

SHE AWAKENED to a persistent jangling coming from her bedside table.

Startled, she sat up and scooped her hair away from her face, then scrambled to reach the phone in time.

"This is Sheriff Wade Montgomery, calling you about that fender."

Her initial panic at hearing the word *sheriff* faded. "And?"

"Never would've expected the results back in a week, but I indicated that this was part of a murder investigation, and they got right on it. If you have a fax out there, I could send a copy of the report."

Disappointed, she sagged against her pillows. "There's one at the clinic, but not here."

"We-e-el, if you've got a pencil handy, you can jot this down, and you can pick up a copy of the report here at the office anytime." He cleared his throat. "Traces of something called *ocean green* were on that fender. The techs found it only in that one narrow gouge we saw. It was *not* a previous layer of color on the fender."

"So what is that exactly?"

"They tell me it's a metallic, deep blue-green, one that would sparkle quite a bit in the sun. Apparently it wasn't very popular, because the company stopped making it eight years ago."

She sat up straighter. "So now we know the vehicle's color, which has to be unique to certain models and years, right? You can locate the vehicle and its owner?"

The long pause on the other end of the line warned her even before Wade spoke. "This color was never a car manufacturer's proprietary stock item."

"And that means?"

"It isn't exclusive to a make and model. It was made by a small company in Utah and sold across the country, Kristin. There's no way to identify a make, model and year through any registration database. I'm sorry, but unless someone has seen a vehicle like that and can give us a clue, we've hit a dead end."

AFTER MOVING CATTLE into the south pasture all morning, Ryan took a shower and went to the office to get to work, though his thoughts were mostly on Kristin and the kiss they'd shared under the stars.

He'd never intended to go this far. Had never wanted to make connections that would hurt her when he had to leave. But every last bit of resolve disappeared when he spent time with her, and now…he was starting to have trouble even imagining a future without her in his arms.

But he had nothing to offer her. Nothing long-term. He'd failed in so many ways. Here at the ranch, when he hadn't measured up to his father's standard. In the service, where he'd failed to save all those children in the hospital explosion. With her, when she'd abandoned him in college.

He'd be leaving the Four Aces soon. There was nothing for him here—certainly not the ranch. Where he went next was anybody's guess, but Kristin and her son had roots here.

He just needed to concentrate on that fact before they went any farther down a road that would only hurt her when he left. Tonight, maybe…

Garrett wandered into the office and perched on the edge of the desk, watching Ryan sort through the current bills and the invoices that would need to go out in the mail.

"Felt pretty dang good to be on a horse again," Garrett said, gingerly testing his ribs. "Three weeks on foot and I was about goin' stir-crazy."

Shoving aside his melancholy thoughts, Ryan rocked back in his chair. "Tell me you aren't going off to some rodeo again this weekend."

"Okay, I'm not." Garrett shrugged.

Ryan raised a brow. "Now tell me the truth."

"Truth is, Jackhammer took some of the fun out of it for me. Leastways, for now."

"He could've done more than that."

"Yeah, well, I'm thinking I need less excitement in my life." Garrett picked up a horseshoe serving as a paperweight and hefted its weight in one hand. "I've been thinking about getting back into reining horses. Trev has been hauling our halter and pleasure horses, but maybe we could diversify a little."

"Sounds like a plan."

Garrett regarded him through narrowed eyes. "So what about you? And don't tell me you're going back into the service. I've *seen* you gimp around in the morning, and that knee isn't going to take you into active combat. Not your shoulder, either."

"Seems there's a lot of people pretty eager to tell me that, but nothing has changed." Ryan pointedly swiveled his chair to face the computer screen and got to work.

"You could take a medical discharge and stay here."

"Right. Dad certainly would be thrilled."

"We could sure use you." Garrett pushed off from the desk and strolled toward the door. "And just think about that pretty little neighbor. I have a feeling she wouldn't mind having you on this side of the world."

Clint walked in just minutes after Garrett walked out. "What's this about you convincing Garrett to quit rodeo?"

"No idea." Ryan spared Clint a brief glance, then continued adding a list of numbers.

"He says you finally made him 'see the dangers of rodeo' and he's going to start training reining horses instead."

Ryan laughed. "My little brother is matchmaking, I think."

Clint looked at him blankly.

"He wants me to stay here. He wants you and me to get along so that can happen."

Harrumph. Clint rifled through the stack of bills on the desk, tapped them into a neat pile.

"Crazy, huh?" Clint didn't answer. "Another crazy thing around here is that you're wrong about Nate Cantrell—at least in part—and you don't want to admit it."

"I'm not going to argue. It's been analyzed six ways to Sunday."

"Maybe so, but hiding your head in the sand doesn't make something right. And if you're all so sure, why did Leland ask me to report anything I found that was unusual? I'd guess you both still have questions." Ryan reached into a desk drawer and pulled out an accordion file tied with a string, and dropped it on the desk with a thud. "Just look at this."

Belatedly, he realized what he'd said to a man whose vision was failing, and he added in a softer tone, "I've now gone through everything I can find from the last four years—so two of those years predate Nate. I've got falsified invoices here. Withdrawals that don't make sense. Some cancelled checks that don't match the invoices or even their own stubs."

Clint reached for the file, then his hand dropped back to his side, his jaw working.

"I've tried to talk to you about this before, Dad. So what do you want to do about it? Cody Cantrell is convinced his grandpa is a criminal. Since Nate's death, there's been gossip about him, and that hurts both the boy and his mom."

"You're saying that an accountant, a P.I. and a lawyer *all* lied? You waltz in here, tell me I've been played for a fool for years?" Clint's voice rose, with an angry and defensive edge. "I always go with the sure bet…the opinions of people I *trust*."

Ryan stared back at him, the finality of Clint's words hitting like rifle fire. Well aimed and deadly. "Then I guess that says it all, Dad." He pushed away from the desk and rose to his feet. "*You* work on these invoices for a while. I'm going for a long walk to clear my head, and then I'll work on moving up my own plans. I should be able to get out of here in three weeks, if not two."

CLINT SAT AT THE DESK and wearily rubbed his eyes, knowing he couldn't work on the books even if he wanted to. It was awful getting old. Worse, to see his independence fading and his world gradually crumbling around his feet.

What if the embezzler *had* been Oscar? Ryan was right about the financial mess predating Nate's arrival, but Clint's greater worry had been over Garrett.

Clint had let the boy go his own way, giving him free rein with those rodeos and the space and freedom to finally grow up and fulfill all of his promise as a Gallagher. But the boy had been perpetually in debt since the age of eighteen, and had been caught with his hand in the cookie jar more than once.

Over the past few years Clint had had suspicions, but hadn't realized the full extent of the losses until after Nate died. Maybe all *three* had betrayed Clint's trust, but it was too late to change a thing.

Whatever happened, he knew there'd be no recovery of the money. And either way, the situation illustrated his own appalling, downward slide. The need to hand over the reins of the family corporation before it was too late.

Picking up the phone, he speed dialed Leland's local office. After reaching only a recording, he tried Leland's cell phone, then his main office in San Antonio.

The secretary—an old battle-ax who'd been with him longer than she should have—announced that Leland was out of town, but would return the call as soon as he could.

Clint glared at the receiver, fighting the temptation to pitch it against the wall.

So much of his life was changing, he felt as if he were teetering on the brink of an abyss with no one to pull him back.

According to Adelfa, Reverend Holden had suffered a massive stroke just yesterday morning, and no one in town knew if he was even going to make it. Yet last Sunday, he'd delivered one of his longest sermons ever, as if he had all the strength in the world. The news had chilled Clint to the bone.

But his own life would soon get back to normal.

He'd already put in a call to a doctor in Austin, who would know where Lydia could go for more experimental treatments. Ryan, with his insistent notions about Nate and the ranch books, would soon be gone. Garrett was finally coming around to the right way of thinking.

And—in a few months—it would be time to

declare for the upcoming Senate campaign and one more term in office.

A man had to take control and make things happen. It was as simple as that.

RAEJEAN, NORA AND CODY arrived back at Cedar Grove Farm just minutes after Kristin showered and dressed on Saturday morning.

Cody burst into the house and dropped his duffel bag on the floor, then flew over to Kris and nearly tackled her with a good-morning hug. "Wow, Mom. That was sooo cool! We went riding, and it was *dark* out. The moon and stars were so bright we could see everything. And then we had a cookout way up on a hill, and we could see the glow of the lights clear over to San— San—"

"San Antonio," Nora said, stepping into the living room with RaeJean at her heels. "You've got quite a cowboy here. Good little rider."

Cody beamed at Nora over his shoulder. "My horse was Pancho, and he *bucked*. And I didn't even fall off!"

"Oh, my." Kristin hugged him back, savoring his warmth and vibrant excitement, thankful he'd had a good time with his two great-aunties. "Then again, you come from good ranching stock. The Cantrells go way back in this county."

"Yeah. How many kids have aunts who ride like that? Even Aunt *RaeJean!*"

His incredulity was so over the top that RaeJean laughed. "He's thinking that a Texas woman can't be decorative and capable at the same time. Little does he know."

"So it went well?"

"Every minute." Nora's voice turned wistful. "Would have been nice to have a few little cow-pokes running around at my spread all these years. You be sure and send him over anytime."

"Do you two have time for coffee? I can make some in a flash."

RaeJean shook her head. "Carlita opened the shop for me this morning, but I've got late-morning appointments."

Nora nodded. "And I've got to take RaeJean back to her place so she can get her car, then I've got to pick up a colt in Llano."

Kristin followed them out to Nora's pickup. "I can't thank you enough for taking care of Cody. It gave him a chance to get to know you two better, and I think he loved every minute."

"Not any more than we did," RaeJean said. "You can be real proud of that boy."

Kristin hesitated, knowing RaeJean's propensity for gossip. "If I ask you something, can you keep it between the three of us?"

"Of *course*," RaeJean exclaimed.

"A while back, you told me some details about

my father's car crash, Nora. You mentioned thinking that you knew who was responsible."

Nora hitched a shoulder. "Weeellll…I have my suspicions, is all. Can't throw a cat in any direction and not hit someone who figures Clint Gallagher pulls the strings in this county."

"I needed more to go on than hearsay, so I've been doing some research. I found a front fender from Dad's truck at Buddy's Auto Shop."

RaeJean's hand went to her mouth. "Oh, my."

"The truck itself is gone, but this fender shows marks on it—possibly, paint residue from a vehicle that *might* have run Dad off the highway."

"Like I always thought," Nora said, her mouth a grim line.

"Trouble is, the residue isn't from an original paint job. If it was, maybe the sheriff could've checked VIN numbers and manufacturer records, and at least come up with a list of possibilities. Someone repainted this car a dark, sea green."

Nora's brow furrowed. "The Four Aces trucks have always been black, same with Clint's Lincolns. That oldest boy has a silver truck, but he hasn't been around all that long."

RaeJean nodded. "In a town this size, we'd probably remember an unusual color like that, but I can't think of a single one. The Bates boys race fancy stock cars, but they paint theirs bright yellow, with loads of emblems plastered everywhere."

Kristin gave each of them a farewell hug. "Thanks anyways. If you think of anything, just give me a call."

Maybe her aunts hadn't seen the car in question, but she was closer to finding out the truth, she could *feel* it. Soon she'd be able to clear her father's name and he could finally rest in peace.

Her mood lifted as she remembered the evening ahead. After going out for dinner with Ryan twice, she'd offered to make him dinner here instead.

She'd picked up flowers for the table yesterday, along with new tapers and dusty rose placemats. The flank steaks were already marinating in her favorite bourbon and honey mixture, and soon she'd need to start on the twice-baked potatoes and banana cream pie.

A quiet evening here would be lovely, and after Cody went to sleep, they could turn on the stereo and dance out in the moonlight. This would be another wonderful evening with him, building another memory to savor.

As much as she'd tried to convince herself otherwise, this was not a friendship. She wasn't just falling in love…she'd never stopped, despite the heartbreak of years past.

And if her wishes came true, maybe it wouldn't have to end.

CODY HAD LONG SINCE gone to bed, and the dishwasher was humming. Candlelight flickered in the darkened living room, mirroring the dying flames in the fireplace.

Ryan brushed a lock of hair behind Kristin's ear, feeling inestimable sadness as he looked into her lovely face. Her skin glowed in the dim light, her eyes were dark and luminous and soft.

"That was the best meal I've had in years," he murmured. "You are amazing."

"It's the Cantrell family's secret marinade. Guys fall for it every time." Her eyes twinkled. "Just wait until you try the pie. You'll be my slave forever."

"It's not the marinade I'm falling for." A warning bell clanged in the far reaches of his brain, but he found himself moving closer and pulling her into a kiss that seemed to wrap around his heart.

Whatever had gone wrong in his life—whatever mistakes he'd made or the ways he'd failed—she was the one true thing. The one person he needed more than life itself. And somehow they were going to work this out, because he could no longer imagine life without her.

No matter what that warning bell was saying.

CHAPTER NINETEEN

AFTER A TENSE Sunday dinner with Ryan and Adelfa, Clint took his coffee into his study, happy to escape Ryan's attempts at polite conversation and Adelfa's reproving glances.

When his private line rang he nearly didn't pick it up, but a glance at the caller ID on the cordless phone base revealed Leland's number. He grabbed the receiver and paced over to the bank of windows facing thousands upon thousands of acres of Four Aces land.

The view usually filled him with a sense of peace. But not this time.

"Clint...sorry I didn't get back to you right away. I've been reviewing the reports from the investigator and the accountant I hired last spring. It's water under the bridge, Clint. You'll never see that money again because Oscar screwed up and Nate is dead."

"I'm well aware of it," Clint snapped. "And that's what all of us have believed. But Ryan has gone back into the records much further. He says significant problems existed long before Cantrell came on board."

"You hired the best—a forensic accountant with a great track record and a respected P.I.—and they did their jobs. They're *experts,* Clint. They spent months doing exactly what you paid them to do."

"Maybe they didn't do it well enough."

Leland snorted. "Your son may have gotten a business degree, but ask yourself what he's been doing with his life. Not accounting. Not investigating white-collar crime."

"He can still run a calculator."

"He's spent his life in the *service.*" The impatience in Leland's voice grew. "Trevor and Garrett wanted him here to help run the ranch office for a while, but he obviously isn't capable of seeing the big picture. Given the way he defied you and walked out on this ranch years ago, maybe he just wants to stir up some trouble before he goes."

Clint shifted uncomfortably as that final, heated argument with Ryan came back to him. Ryan's fury, his promise to never return. Clint's own scathing promise that Ryan would never inherit a blade of grass on Four Aces.

The past still festered between them—unmentioned, unresolved. Ryan had said as much on his first day back in August. "I don't know. I don't think he'd go that far."

"No? Then remember the revised will you had

me draw up. I'm sure he always expected to be a wealthy man someday, and now he'll be living on a service disability pension. Hell, for all we know, he could be finagling a way to use these accusations for his own benefit."

Clint gripped the phone tighter.

"Look, my specialty is law, not accounting or business management. Maybe you should bring in another team to go over everything, just to settle things in your mind. I've got contacts in Dallas who could make some recommendations."

"Let me think about it."

Rubbing at his forehead where a headache was starting to pulse, Clint exhaled slowly. He hadn't wanted to face the possibility that Garrett could have had a part in all that had gone wrong. And now, he felt the same about Ryan. Surely he'd raised his sons to be better men than that. Or had he?

Long after Leland hung up, he stared out the window going back over his life. He'd built the largest ranch in the county. Built it from *nothing*. He'd become a major force in the State Senate during his long political career.

Yet he'd failed at what should matter most to a man—his marriage and the children who should have been his most enduring legacy.

But his marriage was over and his boys were grown, and now it was too late to change a thing.

AFTER A FEW HOURS of work in his office—which amounted to frustration rather than progress— Clint paced through the house, wishing Lydia was around to talk to.

She dropped in now and then, breezy as ever, as if nothing was wrong, though she usually stayed at Trevor's place. Her car had been by the barns earlier, and he'd thought about going down to see her, but then the phone had rung and he'd ended up on a long conference call.

That call had brought into sharp focus one of the things he admired most about Lydia. She'd always been direct as any man at cutting to the heart of an issue, but unlike those in his professional life, she never hesitated to say exactly what was on her mind. She was, he recalled with grudging admiration, the one person who didn't give a damn what he thought.

He could have used her opinion, after his encounter with Ryan this morning. When had everything gone so terribly wrong in this family? When had Ryan become his enemy instead of his son?

At a light rap on the front door he turned, and his heart lifted when he saw her walking in.

She strolled toward him, with the nonchalant grace he'd once loved. "What a surprise. You aren't at your desk making monumental decisions about...something?"

And she still had her talent for veiled sarcasm, as well, obviously. "Good to see you, Lydia."

She gave a throaty laugh. "My, I guess it pays to be terminal."

A sour feeling settled in his stomach. "I'd rather you didn't joke about something that holds so little humor."

"Then for you, I will be exceedingly grim." She moved to the other end of the foyer and scanned the formal living room beyond, as if memorizing each detail. "I've always loved that room. The afternoon light hits it exactly right. But," she added with a regretful sigh, "that isn't why I came up to see you."

She touched a button on the wall and Adelfa appeared a moment later, beaming at the sight of Lydia.

"Yes, ma'am?"

"Could you bring us coffee, please? The library would be fine."

After Adelfa soundlessly disappeared down the hall, Lydia caught the crook of Clint's arm and sauntered to the library, where she let him go to prop a hip against the dark cherry desk. "Ryan tells me he's leaving."

"That's his choice." The angry words erupted before he even took time to think.

"Still fighting the same old battles...and the

biggest loser will be you. Aren't you ever going to give up?"

Moments ago he'd been wishing he had her for a sounding board. Now he was having second thoughts. "Give up what? Having standards? Raising my family to be responsible?"

She shook her head, a hint of amusement playing at the corners of her mouth. "In case you haven't noticed, your children have grown. They're adults, Clint. Probably hopelessly damaged by what we put them through, but they're adults, and the playing field has changed."

"I still own this ranch. I make the decisions."

Lydia flipped her hand, bored. "And you're the big honcho senator and king of the universe. But you won't take any of that to the grave with you, dear. It's time we both tried to put things right."

He opened his mouth, then snapped it shut.

"I may be dying of cancer," she added, "but you could have a heart attack tomorrow and beat me to it. What would you leave behind—other than the obvious tangibles? One of us is going to tell the boys what happened all those years ago, because it's only fair to them. Perhaps we should tell them together."

"I did the *right* thing. I did it for them," he growled, shrugging off a niggling doubt. "You didn't care about them—you were off gallivanting everywhere…and then there was Harris." The name still felt like lye on his tongue.

"Harris? He was just a classmate when I was in graduate school, for heaven's sake, and he's my business partner now. He was never more than that. I love him—and his partner, Edward—like brothers." Her cool veneer faded, leaving just haunting sadness in her huge dark eyes. "I told you the truth, but you wouldn't ever believe me. You chose to assume the worst."

Clint closed his eyes. He'd been consumed with jealousy over Harris, and when he'd finally gotten up the courage to confront her, he hadn't been able to accept her words. The other man's sophistication and education had too easily eclipsed Clint's hardscrabble roots during those early years.

"Do you know why we failed with each other? Do you know why you and Ryan are forever at odds?"

She and Ryan had both been defiant. Outspoken. Independent to a fault, but it would do no good to dredge up those flaws now. She was dying and Ryan was leaving, and soon there would be an empty place in his life that no one else could fill.

"It's because the three of us are *exactly* alike. Too strong, too opinionated, too intelligent to be fooled. Too unwilling to bend. Indomitable forces that were never in agreement about anything."

Adelfa brought in a tray of coffee and set it on a side table, then quietly shut the door as she left.

Lydia went over to the tray and gave Clint a cup, then took one herself. "Do you remember Ryan when he was a little boy? If he set his sights on doing something, he couldn't be swayed. He lost a new kite up in a tree one spring. You'd just bought it for him and you were *furious*. You ordered him to the house, but he went right back outside and worked at getting that kite down for over an hour, because it was too far out on those high, fragile branches for him to reach. He wouldn't give up, and when he fell out of the tree with the kite in his hands, he broke his wrist. He was six years old."

"Why didn't you stop him?"

"I was making supper at the time, and didn't realize he'd gone back outside. Trevor spilled the beans while we were waiting at the E.R." She set her coffee aside. "It was always like that—you making demands, Ryan being defiant. I heard about what happened with the Cantrell girl back when he was in college, by the way, so I know why Ryan left Texas and never moved back."

The room felt warmer. The collar of Clint's shirt felt itchy and tight. "I did the right thing then, too. She was wrong for him. Wrong for this family."

"Wrong for you and your political ambitions, you mean. You thought Kristin wasn't good enough for Ryan because of her father, yet you hired the man a dozen years later."

"Being hired on is hardly the same as forming a permanent family connection," Clint snapped.

Lydia sighed wearily. "I need to go lie down awhile. But think about what I've said, because whether you want it or not, I'm going to set the record straight for our sons before I die. And if you're man enough, you'll be there to help me tell them."

"Hi, Sweetie. Is your momma there?"

Cody smiled at the sound of RaeJean's voice. She had weird hair and fingernails like an assassin's weapons, but she was funny and nice, and she'd baked his favorite cookies every time he'd been to her house. "She's out feeding the horses."

RaeJean chuckled. "You can write her a note so you won't forget this, right? I decided to take Friday off and spend a three-day weekend in Fredericksburg with some friends. I'm leaving in a few minutes. I'd just call her later, but my cell phone fell into a shampoo bowl at the salon and it isn't working."

He reached for a pad of paper and a pencil on the kitchen counter. "Yes, ma'am. Ready."

"Okay. She was asking me about a car. A certain color, sort of shiny blue-green? I knew I'd seen one around like that, and I just remembered where. I saw it once on Main Street. It was such a pretty color—like the deepest water of the ocean—that I watched and watched for it to come back through town again. One day it did, and it parked right down the street in front of Leland Havens's office. He's that lawyer in town, you know. Tall, good-looking man."

Cody chewed on the end of the pencil and fidgeted, realizing that this could take a very long time, and he *really* had to go to the bathroom fast before Trevor and Hayden came to pick him up.

"...so I just trotted over there, quick as a jackrabbit, 'cause I thought I saw a For Sale sign in that pretty little car's window. Only it wasn't... it was just the boy's school papers in the back window. Turns out he was the lawyer's nephew, which is why I saw that car a time or two...and just fell in love with it more each time. I haven't seen it in ages, though. That boy said he liked to race it on the back roads, so I expect it's long gone by now. And of course, it might not have been the right shade of green at all."

She fell silent. Then said, "So did you get that, honey? I know your momma wanted to know."

"Uh-huh." *A race car, here in this little town. Cool.* Cody stared down at the blank piece of paper, unsure of what he ought to write down and afraid she'd say every word again if asked. So he said goodbye then dropped the pencil and raced for the bathroom.

He'd tell Mom about the car when he got home from Hayden's house.

HE AND HAYDEN had started being friends because of football, but both of them had gotten sorta tired of it and now they mostly got together just to hang out. When Ryan was around they tossed the football back and forth with him, but there were other cool things at the ranch.

He and Hayden played explorers in the barn's huge loft sometimes. Alien invaders. There were all those kittens, too. Today was the day Target—because of the bull's-eye on her side—would be old enough to take home, which was why Trevor and Hayden had offered to pick him up after school.

But right now, the kittens had all disappeared.

"I'll check the next barn if you want to look in here," Hayden called out. "Then we can go search the cattle sheds."

There were two huge barns with horses in box stalls, but this was Cody's favorite, with its fancy office, and the big glass window that looked out into the riding arena. Ryan was usually easy to find, because he was either working in the office or on a horse in the arena.

Down the long aisle of the barn, the front of

each stall was polished wood paneling halfway up, topped with iron bars so the horses could look out and people could look in. Cody walked along, hopping up and down in front of each one, trying to find the kittens. No luck. Not in the feed room or the hay storage area, either.

Discouraged, he made his way back to the entrance to the barn, where Hayden was waiting. The other boy shook his head. "Your mom didn't give them all away, did she?"

Hayden chewed on his lower lip. "I don't think she'd do that. Geez! I hope not." He raced for the office. "Maybe Ryan will know."

They only found Garrett at the desk. He looked up from some sort of paper he was filling out and grinned at them. "How are you two cowpokes doing?"

"We can't find the kittens *anywhere.*"

Garrett's brow furrowed. "Can't say as I've seen those little rascals lately, either."

Hayden bounced from one foot to the other. "Then where's Ryan or Dad? Maybe they know."

"Ryan's working one of the colts on the trails across the highway. Your dad…last I saw him, he was in here talking to Leland on the phone about new breeding contracts for next spring. Leland's on his way out, so your dad should be around someplace."

"You don't think anyone gave them away, do you?"

"I doubt it." Garrett chuckled. "I think everyone knows how much you and your sister like those cats."

Hayden slumped into one of the big leather chairs in front of the desk, and Cody followed suit, the missing kittens the only thing he could think about.

Until the name *Leland* finally registered. "Uh-oh."

He slithered down in his seat, trying to remember Aunt RaeJean's long message. It was probably *really* important, and both she and Mom would probably be really mad about him forgetting.

"What's wrong, kid?" Garrett smiled at him. "I'm sure the kittens will turn up. Maybe they're out having a hunting lesson with their momma."

"I forgot to tell my mom about that man's race car."

"*What* man? Who has a race car around here?"

Both Hayden and Garrett were looking at him now, and Cody sat up straight, feeling important at having such cool news to share. "The guy with the funny name. Leland. Aunt RaeJean says he has a fast race car, the color of the deep ocean. I was 'sposed to tell Mom, but I didn't write it down and I forgot."

"That's dumb," Hayden scoffed. "Leland doesn't race cars. He's just an old guy."

Hayden hopped out of his chair and headed for the door, then stopped so suddenly that Cody nearly piled into him. "Hey, watch out!"

His cheeks red, Hayden gave him a sharp elbow in the ribs.

Standing in the doorway was a tall man in a suit, and he sure wasn't smiling. "I don't know where you get this sort of information, young man, but it's not true. Not true at all."

CHAPTER TWENTY

LAST SATURDAY, Ryan had asked her out for tonight, and she'd been looking forward to it all week. Not because of the food or the ambience—or the chance to get away from her usual routine on a Friday night.

She'd been looking forward to spending time with Ryan.

But he didn't call during the week or stop by. And at four o'clock today, he'd called the clinic to give his regrets with just a vague mention of a family obligation.

Cody had been so excited about going to Nora's for a long trail ride Kristin couldn't change his plans. So she'd waved goodbye as Nora's truck bounced down the long gravel road to the highway. After rambling around her old house restlessly for an hour, she grabbed her purse and drove into San Antonio to explore the quaint Riverwalk shops.

With Ryan, it would have been fun just walking down the street, people watching and listening to music filter out of the coffee shops. Alone, she felt empty. As if she'd left a big part of herself behind.

It wasn't, she admitted, a welcome revelation. In less than eight weeks Ryan would be leaving and taking her heart with him, something she'd wanted very much to avoid.

By ten o'clock she'd driven back to Nora's ranch to pick up Cody, and now the two were back on their front porch.

Vaguely uneasy, she tested the door first— locked tight—then peered through the glass into the darkened living room. Everything was just as it should be, with nothing out of place—the TV and stereo undisturbed. Even her digital camera was still perched on the fireplace mantel.

Just your imagination. She stepped inside and flipped on the lights with her hand on the cell phone in her bag.

"Can I stay up and watch a movie?" Cody pleaded. "It's Saturday night!"

"Bedtime, kiddo—soon as you take your bath."

"Aaaw, mom!" But despite his apparent misery, she'd seen him yawning all the way home and knew he was tired.

"You and Nora rode for three hours while I was gone. I'll bet that bed of yours will feel mighty good tonight."

After putting away her groceries, she checked the lock on the back door and turned out the kitchen light, then headed to the den, while Cody filled the tub.

An unexpected, cool draft wafted over her stocking feet as she touched the door. Hesitant, she pushed it open and took a half step back. Across the room, the lace curtains swayed fitfully on the night breeze.

At a window she *always* closed before she left home.

She instinctively took another step back and grabbed her cell phone, hitting the speed dial for 911 in horror.

There was no sign an intruder was still here.

But she'd set up a small home office in the corner of the room, and the filing cabinet hung open and askew. Papers were strewn everywhere.

It hadn't been the wind, and it clearly hadn't been some stray animal after food. Someone had been searching for something.

And if she'd scared him away by arriving late at night, then that person might come back.

SHE REACHED CODY just before he stepped into the bathtub, and ordered him back into his clothes, pronto.

He regarded her with frightened eyes. "Why?"

"We'll be fine, honey. I just think that someone might have been here while we were gone. I've already called 911, so the sheriff or his deputy should be here soon."

After debating the wisdom of going back out in the dark and locking themselves in her truck, she figured they were safer inside the house.

Keeping him at her side, she double-checked the locks on every door and window, shutting every blind and switching on all of the lamps until the house was ablaze with light. Then she stood with him in the living room, her heart hammering in her chest.

She managed a smile. "Kind of an adventure, don't you think?"

He shrugged. "Can I watch TV now?"

The resiliency of childhood made her laugh. "Yes, you can. Just keep it really low, okay?"

He put in one of his favorite DVDs and turned on the TV, while she listened for sounds that shouldn't be there, and prayed that their intruder had long since headed over the hills.

Within ten minutes the welcoming wail of a siren came up the highway, and soon flashing lights were spinning across the hillsides, painting them an eerie shade of red. A second patrol car arrived moments later.

Her heart still pounding, Kristin looked gratefully out at the circus of strobe lights and vehicles, then bent to give Cody a loving squeeze. "See, honey? We're fine."

He flipped off the TV and went to stand at the windows, his eyes wide. "Wow!"

Wade dispatched his deputy to search her house while he started taking a report from Kristin.

"Any ideas at all?" Wade asked, after taking down general information. "Anyone say anything to you—threaten you in any way?"

"No one." She smiled at Cody. "Maybe you should go sit on the sofa for a while and watch your movie. You don't want to miss the best part, right?"

She waited until Cody left, then lowered her voice. "I haven't had any personal threats, Sheriff. I don't owe anyone money. I haven't had any bad business deals. There've been no difficult patients at the clinic to speak of. I've been looking into my Dad's death, but only you, my aunts and I know about the fender, and that the report came back."

"Have you talked to any locals about the accident? Made anyone edgy?" Wade frowned as he jotted notes on his clipboard.

"Max at the clinic knows I've been working on this, but he's newer in town than I am. Buddy...but he could've hidden that fender instead of giving it to me, so he's just been helpful. And Ryan—but he's trustworthy."

Wade looked at her sharply. "You told a *Gallagher*?"

"Inadvertently...sort of."

"Ma'am, if someone was after your father, who would be the most likely suspect?"

Clint Gallagher. But how could she be sure of that…and how could she explain that the man's eldest son was different? "I…I'm working on it."

The deputy came back with his own clipboard and frowned at Wade. "Just as she said, boss. I found TVs, a DVD player and a digital camera, all in plain sight. A jewelry box on her dresser upstairs, and it didn't look like anyone had pawed through it. But the den—the suspect was trying real hard to find something in those files." He turned his attention to Kristin. "Any idea what he was looking for?"

"Money? Credit cards?"

"Then he would have taken small valuables, too. We'll check for fingerprints, but that's a long shot—local troublemakers wouldn't be in the system, and a pro would wear gloves. If you can figure out what's missing—or what someone tried to find—we'll have a better chance."

She shivered as she met and held Wade's gaze. "Evidence about my dad's accident?"

He nodded. "Given the circumstances, that's my guess, too. Now we need to figure out who might have been driving that car."

KRISTIN LEFT all the lights blazing for the rest of the night. Long after Cody went to sleep, she worked through the papers that had been thrown about in the den.

The deputy was right. A random burglar would have taken valuables. Someone was after specific information, but the range of possibilities was frighteningly narrow.

Ted certainly wasn't after anything to prove her less than competent as a mother—he wasn't particularly happy about Cody's weekend stays anyway and had never pushed for full custody.

No one could imagine, looking around at her spare furnishings and the condition of the house, that she would have secret treasures hidden away. Even in these days of identity theft and credit card fraud, surely a thief would pick on someone who appeared much more affluent.

And that left the possibility that her father's killer knew about her quest...and wanted to either frighten her or take whatever proof she might have found.

Buddy and Wade had been nothing but helpful. Nora and RaeJean were certainly trustworthy... though RaeJean had a penchant for gossip and didn't always get her facts straight, so she might have inadvertently said something to the wrong person.

And then there was Ryan. A man she'd loved all these years, whether she'd admitted it to herself or not. But what would he have to gain? The truth hit her like a fist slamming into her stomach, taking her breath away.

Millions.

She sat back on her heels. Years ago, he'd defied his father because of her. He'd lost his inheritance, his future at the Four Aces and his close family ties. Now, facing the possibility of permanent disability and the end of his military career, wouldn't he want to regain the good graces of his father?

And if Clint had caused her father's death, there would be no better way than to stay close to her, keep close tabs on what she discovered and then find a way to eliminate that evidence. Or give her a warning.

He'd canceled their date. Perhaps he'd watched the house, hoping she would leave.... But surely she couldn't have been so wrong about him.

She leaned against her desk and stared at the wall...and wondered if she'd been a fool after all.

"CAN WE GO OVER to the ranch, Mom?" Cody begged on Saturday morning, around a mouthful of his favorite chocolate-chip pancakes. "I bet I can find the kittens. Please?"

"Actually, I got a call from Hayden's dad this morning." Kristin refilled his glass of milk. "They did find Target, and said they'll drop her off around four this afternoon on their way out of town."

But she hadn't heard a word from Ryan...which seemed so strange.

"Hayden's going away again?" Cody's face fell. "I wanted to go over there to play, or maybe have him come here this time."

She ruffled his hair. "Sounds like they'll be pretty busy. They're packing up for a horse show in Dallas, and I hear Hayden and his sister have to help pack their motor home. Maybe there's someone else at school you can call."

"Na-a-ah." He pushed the rest of his pancakes around in the sea of syrup on his plate.

"Want to go riding this morning? It's such a pretty day. When we get back, we can get ready for that kitten of yours."

He perked up. "Can we go on the trail across the highway?"

They'd been over there once before, but they'd left too late and dusk had sent them home again before they'd gotten very far. According to Miranda, the trail wound through another parcel of the K-Bar-C land destined for new owners under the Home Free program, but it would be the last area developed. "We should have plenty of time, honey. We could even pack some sandwiches and juice, if you'd like. Help me clear up these dishes, and we'll go."

THE CRISP OCTOBER BREEZE and bright sunshine made every mile a delight, as did the endlessly rolling Hill Country, with vistas waiting around every bend. Kristin could have gone on forever, but by two o'clock in the afternoon, Cody was ready to turn home.

Rebel, who'd trudged patiently down the trail with his nose nearly on the ground and his ears at half-mast, was a different horse the moment they turned back. Ears pricked, head high, he eased into a fast walk that kept Boots at an intermittent jog just to keep up.

"I think he must be hungry," Cody said, laughing.

"Rebel is *always* hungry."

"Can we lope? I bet he'd really go, now!"

Kristin shook her head. "He's a sweetheart, but I'd hate to have him get away from you. That highway is coming up."

Cody dutifully slumped back down in his saddle.

She watched him ride. He was so much more confident now and so much happier than he'd been when they first moved to Homestead. Whatever else she had to deal with here, this move had been a good one for him. A place to put down roots, with his great-aunts close by and the wide open spaces offering a taste of freedom, a departure from the urban life they'd had before.

When they reached their driveway, Cody kicked Rebel into a slow jog and rounded the last bend. A second later, she heard a whoop of delight.

"They're here, Mom! They came!"

By the time she caught up, Cody had dismounted and tied his horse to the hitching rail, and had run over to the Gallagher's motor home parked in front of the house.

Garrett stood leaning against a front fender, his legs crossed at the ankles. "Afternoon, ma'am," he said. "Looks like we made someone's day."

Wearing the biggest smile she'd ever seen, Cody already had the kitten in his arms. "Isn't she beautiful, Mom?"

"It sure was nice of you to stop by." Kristin dismounted and led Boots over to Garrett. "I'm sorry you had to wait for us. You're probably in a hurry."

"I got here a little early." Garrett shrugged. "No problem. Trevor and the rest of them went on ahead with the big rig, because we figured it might be too tight to turn it around down here."

"What do you say, Cody?" Kristin prompted.

"Thanks a *million!* Target is the coolest kitten ever!"

Garrett grinned back at him and touched the brim of his hat. "I think so, too." He opened the door of the motor home, climbed behind the wheel and switched on the ignition. Resting the crook of his elbow in the open window, he winked at Cody. "A whole lot cooler than having any ole green race cars, right?"

In a cloud of dust, he headed up the lane.

"What did he mean by that?" Kristin asked casually, leaning down to scratch the kitten gently behind one ear.

Cody's gaze veered away. "Nuthin'."

His sudden edginess told her that wasn't exactly true. "Nothing?"

He put the kitten back in its carrying cage. "We were just joking around."

He went over to the hitching rack and began unsaddling his horse. She watched him struggle with the girth, then went over to help him. With a few deft tugs she released the long latigo strap and hauled the saddle off, handing Cody the saddle blanket.

"It wasn't true anyway," he muttered, his lower lip stuck out in a pout reminiscent of his preschool days. "Hayden thought I was stupid."

She untied Rebel and led the horse into the corral, let him loose, then went to unsaddle Boots. "What's not true?"

"About that green car?"

"Exactly."

He stubbed his toe in the dirt, the tips of his ears reddening. "I was 'sposed to tell you, but I forgot."

She took a deep breath to curb her exasperation. "Who told you, Cody? *When?*"

"Aunt RaeJean called. She told me about a green car that someone races. She saw it in town once."

"Whose car was it, Cody?"

"It wasn't true, anyway." He was looking up at her warily now, as if he'd realized just how much he'd screwed up, and his voice was defensive. "She said it belonged to a kid who raced it sometimes. I thought it was sorta cool, so I told Hayden. But that crabby lawyer—the one who goes over to Hayden's a lot—was there, and he heard me. And he said it was a lie."

Kristin took a sharp breath as the possibilities became all too clear. She tried for an easy smile. "How on earth would he know that?"

"Because RaeJean said he was the kid's uncle."

IT ALL FELL INTO PLACE. The Gallagher's lawyer. Ryan's attentive behavior. The break-in after Ryan had coincidentally canceled their date on Friday night.

Ryan had probably told his father about the '67 Chevy's fender, and Clint had been stewing about it ever since.

If Clint had set up her father's murder, he certainly wouldn't want any possible proof to surface, but the big question was why he would have wanted Nate dead while the money was still missing.

What would it gain? If Nate had supposedly embezzled money, his death would preclude any possibility that he could be forced to either reveal its location or make restitution.

None of this made sense, but dwelling on it kept her from accepting the painful truth that she'd been played for an absolute fool.

As soon as she got the horses put away and settled Cody in the house with his kitten, she stepped out onto the porch with her cell phone and left a message with the secretary at the sheriff's office.

Wade returned her call minutes later, his voice worried. "Is everything all right out at your place?"

"Believe me, I would've called 911 if there was trouble." She hesitated, knowing it was a long shot. "RaeJean remembers seeing someone driving a blue-green car similar to the color I described. She saw it a couple of times."

"Do you have a name? License plate?"

Kristin paced across the porch, her stomach tightening. "No...but she thought the boy was one of Leland Havens's nephews."

He fell silent. "He could have a different last name."

"I know."

"And it could be a totally different color, not a match at all."

"Right."

"And even if it's a match, the car could have been sold, repainted or junked by now. Just finding this person would be no guarantee."

The futility made her stomach tighten even more. "You don't think it's worth checking out?"

"It's absolutely worth pursuing, if this was a homicide." Wade's voice was hard. "Leland lives in San Antonio, but I think most of his people come from around here. I'll see if I can get some names."

She rested her head against one of the support posts on the porch. "Thank you."

"It's my job. And Kristin, I promise to keep the case open until we find answers."

She leaned against the post listening to Cody playing with his kitten. Such innocence…such joy in simple things.

It was hard to imagine ever feeling that carefree again.

But no one at the Four Aces knew anything had changed. Clint would still assume he controlled the universe and everyone in it. The lawyer would assume he'd outsmarted the law by borrowing a different car…and whoever had driven it would still be sure they'd gotten away with murder.

And Ryan—unless she listened to the small

voice in her heart—was still sure she'd fallen for his ruse.

Garrett had mentioned that "Trevor and the rest of them" had gone to Dallas, so this might be the perfect time to drop over and ask a couple of the Four Aces ranch hands some questions. Flipping open her phone again, she speed dialed Nora and asked if Cody could come over for a couple hours.

The Four Aces was no longer a safe place for him, right now. But with a little luck, she might stumble across some leads that could prove who killed her father.

CHAPTER TWENTY-ONE

CLINT RUSTLED the *Dallas Daily News,* tried to focus on the fine print, then slammed it down on the table. The headlines wavered and the articles were impossible to read.

The inexorable progression of his macular degeneration had been a slow and cunning thing. Insidious, lulling him into the belief that he would overcome it just as he'd overcome every other obstacle in his life.

But sheer defiance wouldn't change the inevitability of this disease, and the prospect terrified him.

He pushed away from the table, his anger simmering and his blood pounding in his temples. What was he going to do with the rest of his life—stare off into nothing? Be as useless as a baby, needing care? Listen to the sympathetic whispers of people he would never see?

He stalked down the hallway, then realized he had nowhere to go. No business he could do. No books he could read.

Adelfa had gone to Saturday evening mass and

the rest of them had gone to the show in Dallas, far as he knew. His footsteps rang hollow on the terrazzo flooring of the empty house—echoing exactly what he would become. Alone, hollow. Without purpose.

In the living room, he paused in front of the fireplace and looked up at the indistinct shadow, displayed in a custom, mahogany-framed case, that had been his grandfather's gun. A sleek 1800s Allen & Wheelock Army revolver, it was worth close to eight grand when last appraised.

Worth more, perhaps, as a way to end a bleak future, if the thing even worked.

Somewhere outside a dog barked, and tires crunched on the caliche gravel. He went to a window and made out the shape of a car down by the main horse barn. Strange, because no one should be here. The hands usually went into town on Saturday nights, and the family had gone to Dallas.

Probably a customer, he realized, the tension relaxing in his shoulders. Owners often dropped in over the weekend to check on the horses they had in training. Potential buyers from across the country knew the ranch well and occasionally stopped in to look over the show prospects or breeding stock.

Unfortunately, most of them arrived ready for endless conversation about their horses and the latest horse show gossip, while some happily settled into exhaustive debates on particular bloodlines, or—worse, if they happened to encounter Clint—their political gripes. Ad nauseam.

He'd never cared to waste that kind of time.

Growling under his breath, he left the house and headed down to the barn. Oddly enough, the car was empty. The barns were dark. And only a dim light shone in the office—just the small lamp that was left on, day and night.

Who would come out here and go roaming at dusk? He focused again on the office window, indignant, and flipped on the aisle lights as he stepped into the barn.

Then he jerked open the office door and hit the light switches with the heel of his hand. "Who's in here?"

Crouched at the bank of file drawers along the wall, a dark figure in a hooded sweatshirt rose slowly.

Deliberately.

Turned to face him.

Something silver glinted in the faint light—

With a deafening explosion, a deep, burning pain ripped through his chest. Staggering, stunned, he opened his mouth to scream....

And then the room went black.

BY THE TIME KRISTIN dropped Cody off at Nora's, the sky had darkened to a deep purple and she realized she'd probably missed her chance. Most cowboys headed for the honky-tonks or one of the local, out-of-the-way places where you could find great barbecue or Texas-size steaks at mom-and-pop prices.

Still, she decided at the entrance to the Four Aces, you never knew. This could be the *perfect* opportunity. There was usually at least one employee around the barns—probably as a security measure—and maybe he'd come out to her truck and greet her. He might even be glad for the company and less hesitant to answer a few casual questions without anyone else around.

She'd seen the hands who worked at the ranch and had met most of them—middle-aged, thickset, friendly guys. None she'd hesitate to encounter alone. She suspected Clint was very particular about hiring.

She continued up the lane. By the main barn she pulled to a stop under one of several overhead security lights, a dozen yards away from a car parked farther in the shadows. One of the hand's wives, maybe?

The barn's lights were on, as were the office lights…but no one came out. Her initial resolve melted away.

Maybe they *had* all gone to town, simple as that, though finding absolutely no one around was unsettling, and she felt an eerie chill. Instead of getting out of her truck, she hit the locks and rolled her windows most of the way up.

Perhaps someone was working a horse on the other side of the arena…or was tending to chores in another part of the barn, and hadn't heard her arrive. But now coming here seemed like a foolish decision.

Shifting her truck in Reverse, she glanced over her shoulder to start backing up.

At a soft tap on her window, she spun back and found a broad-shouldered figure looming, silhouetted in menacing, featureless black by the security light behind him.

With a scream she jerked away from the window, a hand at her mouth. Her heart hammered wildly.

"Kristin! It's just me. Ryan."

Not reassuring news.

Breathless, she stared at him, finally making out his familiar features. "W-what are you doing here?"

"Well, I live here, for starters," he said. "At least for now."

"You scared me half to *death*."

"I didn't mean to. I figured you were looking for me."

"I—I guess I got here too late. E-everyone's gone…and then you just came out of nowhere." But it wasn't just his sudden appearance that shook her. No longer knowing if she could trust him…wondering if he'd *intended* to scare her, she bit her lip and tried to think of a good excuse for her arrival…and couldn't think of a single one. "I think I'll just head home, after all."

He took a half step back, and she could see his deeply shadowed features. A frown furrowed his brow as he studied her. "I was out putting some miles on a colt and got back a few minutes ago. I thought I heard a strange noise over here."

"I just pulled in, but I didn't hear anything." She hiked a thumb toward the other vehicle, which was now nearly invisible in the deepening shadows. "Maybe they would know."

He looked over the hood of her truck. "I don't know who that could be."

Something about him changed as he scanned the area, then pinned his gaze on that car.

In place of a relaxed cowboy she saw what he must be like in the service, with an air of power and confidence that intimidated as much as any gun.

"You stay here, Kristin. Keep your doors locked. Or better yet, maybe you should go home."

Going home sounded like a very good idea, but something made her hesitate. "What are you going to do?"

"I'm just checking everything out." His mouth curved in a faint grin. "Like night patrol."

Her premonition grew when he stepped into the light of the barn...and shot off the charts when he disappeared inside the office door.

Two minutes passed. Three. Four.

It would have been logical for him to step into the hallway and wave or come out to say goodbye, but ten minutes went by without sight of him.

He could be making a phone call or answering one. He could have settled down to work on some accounts, and won't welcome you making a big scene.

Yet if something was wrong, who else was here to help?

Saying a silent prayer, she pocketed her cell phone and slipped out of her truck, thankful she'd worn her running shoes instead of her hard-soled boots.

The dark shadows beyond the reach of the security lights seemed to pulse with danger.

Her heart took up a staccato beat and her palms grew damp as she crept toward the side of the building, her senses on high alert. Every breath rasped in her throat. Every step seemed to echo in the building complex as she drew closer. Closer.

She eased into the barn, her hands and knees shaking.

A few more steps...just a few...

An angry voice spiraled out of control from

inside the office, then she heard Ryan's soothing tones.

When she leaned over a few inches to peer into the room, she saw why.

A tall man in a hooded shirt stood in the middle of the room with his back to the door. In one trembling hand he held the top of a large black garbage sack overflowing with manila folders. In the other—

Oh, no—he held a *gun*.

And Ryan was in there someplace. *Defenseless*.

Fear turned her blood to ice as she held her breath and eased just a millimeter farther, though every instinct screamed at her to run.

Horror replaced her fear when she blinked and focused on Clint lying in a pool of blood in front of the desk. Ryan knelt next to him, pressing a crimson-soaked cloth to his father's chest.

For just a second, Ryan met and held her eyes, then he almost imperceptibly tilted his head, obviously wanting her to leave.

Clint had been shot. Ryan obviously could see the intruder's face and could identify him. She didn't have to guess at Ryan's chances.

"It's over," Ryan said, his voice low and soothing. "I know it was just an accident, right? You heard a noise. Thought there was an intruder. Self-defense, really… I'm sure the sheriff will see that's all this was. An instinctive reaction. So just put the gun down and take a deep breath. I'll explain it to him...."

Ryan's voice followed her as she eased back out of sight and speed dialed 911. Urgently she whispered a few words into the receiver, then scanned her surroundings frantically.

The barn was perfectly neat as always, nothing out of place.

Her terrified gaze settled on the little utility alcove by her shoulder...but it held only a broom, a flat grain shovel and a plastic pan of dog kibble.

Her heart battering against her ribs, she grabbed the pan and the shovel.

Said another silent prayer.

Then threw the pan far down the aisle, sending kibbles bouncing on the cement like buckshot. She flattened herself into the alcove...praying Ryan could move fast.

In the office, someone shouted.

Footsteps shuffled toward the door. She could see the edge of the unknown man's back and shoulder. She held her breath. *Please...please... please...*

The man took another step backward. Turning only at the waist, the aim of his gun wavered, as he snapped his gaze down the aisle.

His gun wavered a second time.

She lunged forward with the shovel. Hit the back of his knees with every ounce of her strength.

He screamed, falling forward. The gun spun away across the cement.

And at that instant, Ryan burst out of the office and went down on top of him twisting one of the man's arms high behind his back. "I'll take care of this. Please—my father's bleeding. Help him!"

AMIDST THE MELEE of ambulances and police cars, she caught a glimpse of the intruder—his head still covered, but his hands now cuffed behind his back.

Despite the hood, she could still see the glitter of loathing in his eyes as he glared at her.

Then his hood slipped back and exposed his features…and suddenly it all made sense.

"WE CANNOT THANK YOU ENOUGH," Lydia said, pressing her fingers to her throat. "You took a terrible risk, but without you…I can't bear imagining what could have happened."

Kristin checked Clint's sutures, examined the surgical wound for any sign of infection, then applied a new dressing. "I have to admit, my knees still shake when I think about it."

"Leland had no intentions of leaving witnesses," Clint growled.

Clint had been airlifted to the hospital in San Antonio, where he'd had surgery, but after just two days he'd insisted on coming back to the ranch this morning.

"You're doing very well, Mr. Gallagher. You're on powerful antibiotics, which should take care of any infection. But if you start running a fever, chill or have increased pain, make sure you call me right away." She snapped her medical case shut. "Otherwise, I'll be back tomorrow afternoon to check your dressing again."

Lydia followed her into the hall. Her eyes glistened as she took Kristin's hand. "If there's ever anything I can do for you. *Anything.* You must tell me."

The older woman was even more pale than before, her eyes sunken with weariness. "For starters, you need to go rest. I'll bet you sat up with him all night long. I'd guess your health is far more fragile than his."

"Perhaps." A corner of her mouth lifted as she met and held Kristin's gaze. "I can tell by your expression that you realize how ill I am. Ironic, isn't it? He and I spent a lifetime apart, unable to coexist. Now he's wounded and I'm dying, and we've come back together for whatever time we have left."

The poignancy of those lost years touched Kristin. The parallel between their relationship and hers with Ryan was too obvious to ignore. "At least you've got each other now," she said wistfully. "I can see that you love each other. Some of us will never have what you have."

"Sometimes you need to fight for what matters most." Lydia squeezed Kristin's hand, then released it. "Though some of us learn that lesson far too late."

"But for some, love isn't enough. The incompatibilities, different dreams, just lead to heartache."

"Don't be so sure." From the bedroom Clint called out for Lydia. "Wade and Ryan are in the study, dear. I think they want to talk to you before you leave."

Kristin watched her return to Clint's bedside, then went down to the study. Wade and Ryan stood at the window, deep in conversation, but both stopped at her approach.

"We've done quite a bit of investigation over the past couple days," Wade said. He motioned her to a chair and then sat across from her, a folder in his hands. "The district attorney is in the process of filing a long list of charges against Leland—including second-degree murder *and* attempted murder—so you don't need to worry about him going free."

"S-so it was Leland who ran my dad off the road?"

Wade nodded. "I did some checking after I tracked down some Havenses who live around here. Apparently, he borrowed his nephew's car.

Didn't want to use his own in case someone saw him."

"But wasn't it damaged?"

"Yep—but he never turned in a claim. Instead, he gave the kid twice what the car was worth and sold it to a used-car dealer down in Galveston."

She'd thought she would feel a sense of victory if she could prove the circumstances of her father's death. But now she sat back in her chair, stunned and shaky. "He might never have been caught."

"Leland helped Clint find and hire the investigators who examined the Four Aces books, but those guys were in Leland's pocket, from what we can tell." Wade tipped his head toward Ryan. "Leland also covered his thefts by blaming Oscar's 'mismanagement' and Nate's embezzlement."

"I thought Clint and Leland were *friends*."

"Clint thought so too, I guess. He defended the guy to the end, but Ryan was suspicious about a lot of things that didn't add up."

Incredulous, Kristin shook her head. "So it was Leland, then. Not anyone else."

"He wasn't just the ranch lawyer, he was a financial advisor who could oversee and approve contracts or major expenditures while Clint was away. Which was most of the time, given Clint's political career." Wade tapped the file. "He's been a signatory on ranch checks for years, along with Clint and the foreman. Now there are grown sons here to handle things. But when the boys were small, it was a setup Clint needed."

"Leland has been filtering money for years," Ryan added. "He also tricked my father into some phony investment shells and several nonexistent offshore investment schemes—the sort of under-the-table deals a guy like my dad would be happy to use if he could avoid taxes. That aura of secrecy just helped Leland succeed."

"But none of this makes sense. What about my dad?"

Ryan and Wade exchanged glances, then Wade nodded. "I'll let you two talk. I need to visit with Clint for a bit."

"I couldn't figure it out at first, either." Ryan accepted the file from Wade, then pulled up a chair next to her. "So Wade contacted the state authorities. He got a report back about a murder victim found near the Mexican border a number of years ago. Dental records in Homestead were a match for Oscar Ruiz."

She stared at him. "But why?"

"We figure Oscar must have caught on to Leland. Maybe he threatened to tell Clint, or the sheriff. After Oscar 'disappeared,' Leland probably went through the files and covered his own tracks by altering or destroying all the evidence he could find."

"Which is why Oscar held his job as long as he did. He'd been doing fine until his so-called incompetence was discovered later." A wave of sadness engulfed her. "I suppose the same thing happened to my dad."

"Probably." Ryan pulled a sheet of paper from the folder and handed it to her. "But this time, Leland planned ahead. He set up a scheme to frame your father, to cover his own thefts, and hinted that your dad blew all his money on gambling. Then he made sure Nate could never defend himself."

"My dad had nothing," Kristin whispered. "Leland is a *lawyer*. With his career, he could have had anything he wanted."

Ryan shook his head. "Wade thinks he just got in too deep over the years. Fancy home, impressive vacations, debts that overwhelmed him. Who knows? Maybe it was simply greed."

"My father died so Leland could continue enjoying those luxuries." The unfairness was almost beyond bearing. Leland had been caught, but none of this could bring her father back. Handing the paper to Ryan, she rose wearily to her feet. "Thank you for helping clear my dad's name."

"After the criminal trial, you can pursue a civil suit against Leland for wrongful death," Ryan said. "Given all we know, you should be successful."

She felt tears burn beneath her eyelids, but willed them away. "Blood money."

"Security, for Cody's future and your own. You two won't have to worry."

You two won't have to worry.

Nothing had changed. The future wouldn't include Ryan—it was easy enough to read between the lines when she looked into his somber eyes.

Ryan had been a part of her dreams for too long to even remember. But his inevitable departure wasn't far away, and maybe this was the best time to simply say goodbye.

She held out her hand and swallowed hard. "I appreciate all you've done, Ryan. I hope we can stay in touch."

He looked down at her hand, then his eyes locked on hers, and he reached out to touch her chin, tipping her face toward his. The pain and regret in his expression deepened. "I can't imagine anything worse."

She'd already accepted that their relationship would end, but hearing him say those words cut deep.

"Of course. I understand." Embarrassed, she tried to turn away, but he caught her shoulders and brought her back to face him.

"I don't want to just stay in touch. I want another chance at *us*. We lost something very precious, years ago, and I hope it's not too late to give this another try."

"But...you're leaving. You said you never wanted any ties."

He kissed her, long and slow, with heartbreaking tenderness. "And that has been one of my biggest mistakes. I love you, Kristin. I always have, though I was too angry and proud to admit it. Years ago, I believed you walked away because I had nothing left to offer you—no future, no security."

"That wasn't true. Only *you* mattered." But she could never tell him the rest of the story. Not when it seemed he'd finally made peace with his father.

Ryan's eyes were deep with understanding. "My mother explained a lot of things. It'll be hard to ever forgive Dad for threatening your family. Even harder knowing that you and I have wasted so many years because of it."

"He thought he was protecting his own, I guess."

"It was never right, and it wasn't the only time. When he and my mother split up, he threatened to drag her into a mudslinging court battle for as many years as it took, if she dared fight for custody. Rather than put her young kids through all of that, she gave in."

"And gave up everything she loved. Her home, her children."

"Knowing the truth is better than imagining she never cared." Ryan gave her a faint smile. "Now, I guess she's agreed to stay here and take care of him…while he thinks he's going to retire from politics and start taking care of *her.* Should be interesting."

"And you? What will you do now—head back into the service? Ride off into the sunset?"

"Dad wants me to stay on. I know we'll never get along well, but he wants me to be a full partner in this place with him and my brothers. In fact, he made it an *order.*" Ryan laughed. "Given his temperament and mine, I'm definitely thinking about that sunset."

He held Kristin close for a moment before pulling away, his eyes so full of love and tenderness that she felt her own eyes burn.

"All of that seems inconsequential, given the most important thing in my life."

"Which is?"

"This is coming many years too late, but I mean it more than ever, because my poor ole heart isn't going to take another day without you. Marry me, Kris. I'll take Homestead or that sunset— wherever I can be with you."

"This is where we belong. Here. Together," she whispered as she melted into his arms. "And tomorrow couldn't be soon enough."

* * * * *

REQUEST YOUR FREE BOOKS!

2 FREE INSPIRATIONAL NOVELS
PLUS 2
FREE
MYSTERY GIFTS

LARGER-PRINT BOOKS!

GET 2 FREE
LARGER-PRINT NOVELS
PLUS 2 FREE
MYSTERY GIFTS

Love Inspired

Larger-print novels are now available...

YES! Please send me 2 FREE LARGER-PRINT Love Inspired® novels and my 2 FREE mystery gifts (gifts are worth about $10). After receiving them, if I don't wish to receive any more books, I can return the shipping statement marked "cancel". If I don't cancel, I will receive 6 brand-new novels every month and be billed just $4.99 per book in the U.S. or $5.49 per book in Canada. That's a saving of at least 23% off the cover price. It's quite a bargain! Shipping and handling is just 50¢ per book in the U.S. and 75¢ per book in Canada.* I understand that accepting the 2 free books and gifts places me under no obligation to buy anything. I can always return a shipment and cancel at any time. Even if I never buy another book, the two free books and gifts are mine to keep forever.

122/322 IDN FEG3

Name _____ (PLEASE PRINT)

Address _____ Apt. #

City _____ State/Prov. _____ Zip/Postal Code

Signature (if under 18, a parent or guardian must sign)

Mail to the **Reader Service:**
IN U.S.A.: P.O. Box 1867, Buffalo, NY 14240-1867
IN CANADA: P.O. Box 609, Fort Erie, Ontario L2A 5X3

Not valid to current subscribers to Love Inspired Larger-Print books.

**Are you a current subscriber to Love Inspired books
and want to receive the larger-print edition?
Call 1-800-873-8635 or visit www.ReaderService.com.**

* Terms and prices subject to change without notice. Prices do not include applicable taxes. Sales tax applicable in N.Y. Canadian residents will be charged applicable taxes. Offer not valid in Quebec. This offer is limited to one order per household. All orders subject to credit approval. Credit or debit balances in a customer's account(s) may be offset by any other outstanding balance owed by or to the customer. Please allow 4 to 6 weeks for delivery. Offer available while quantities last.

Your Privacy—The Reader Service is committed to protecting your privacy. Our Privacy Policy is available online at www.ReaderService.com or upon request from the Reader Service.

We make a portion of our mailing list available to reputable third parties that offer products we believe may interest you. If you prefer that we not exchange your name with third parties, or if you wish to clarify or modify your communication preferences, please visit us at www.ReaderService.com/consumerschoice or write to us at Reader Service Preference Service, P.O. Box 9062, Buffalo, NY 14269. Include your complete name and address.

LILP11B

REQUEST YOUR FREE BOOKS!

2 FREE RIVETING INSPIRATIONAL NOVELS
PLUS 2 FREE MYSTERY GIFTS

Love Inspired®
SUSPENSE

YES! Please send me 2 FREE Love Inspired® Suspense novels and my 2 FREE mystery gifts (gifts are worth about $10). After receiving them, if I don't wish to receive any more books, I can return the shipping statement marked "cancel". If I don't cancel, I will receive 4 brand-new novels every month and be billed just $4.49 per book in the U.S. or $4.99 per book in Canada. That's a saving of at least 22% off the cover price. It's quite a bargain! Shipping and handling is just 50¢ per book in the U.S. and 75¢ per book in Canada.* I understand that accepting the 2 free books and gifts places me under no obligation to buy anything. I can always return a shipment and cancel at any time. Even if I never buy another book, the two free books and gifts are mine to keep forever.

123/323 IDN FEHR

Name	(PLEASE PRINT)	
Address		Apt. #
City	State/Prov.	Zip/Postal Code

Signature (if under 18, a parent or guardian must sign)

Mail to the Reader Service:
IN U.S.A.: P.O. Box 1867, Buffalo, NY 14240-1867
IN CANADA: P.O. Box 609, Fort Erie, Ontario L2A 5X3

Not valid for current subscribers to Love Inspired Suspense books.

**Are you a subscriber to Love Inspired Suspense
and want to receive the larger-print edition?
Call 1-800-873-8635 or visit www.ReaderService.com.**

* Terms and prices subject to change without notice. Prices do not include applicable taxes. Sales tax applicable in N.Y. Canadian residents will be charged applicable taxes. Offer not valid in Quebec. This offer is limited to one order per household. All orders subject to credit approval. Credit or debit balances in a customer's account(s) may be offset by any other outstanding balance owed by or to the customer. Please allow 4 to 6 weeks for delivery. Offer available while quantities last.

Your Privacy—The Reader Service is committed to protecting your privacy. Our Privacy Policy is available online at www.ReaderService.com or upon request from the Reader Service.

We make a portion of our mailing list available to reputable third parties that offer products we believe may interest you. If you prefer that we not exchange your name with third parties, or if you wish to clarify or modify your communication preferences, please visit us at www.ReaderService.com/consumerschoice or write to us at Reader Service Preference Service, P.O. Box 9062, Buffalo, NY 14269. Include your complete name and address.

LARGER-PRINT BOOKS!

**GET 2 FREE
LARGER-PRINT NOVELS
PLUS 2 FREE
MYSTERY GIFTS**

Love Inspired
SUSPENSE
RIVETING INSPIRATIONAL ROMANCE

Larger-print novels are now available...

REQUEST YOUR FREE BOOKS!

2 FREE INSPIRATIONAL NOVELS
PLUS 2
FREE
MYSTERY GIFTS

Love Inspired
HISTORICAL
INSPIRATIONAL HISTORICAL ROMANCE

YES! Please send me 2 FREE Love Inspired® Historical novels and my 2 FREE mystery gifts (gifts are worth about $10). After receiving them, if I don't wish to receive any more books, I can return the shipping statement marked "cancel". If I don't cancel, I will receive 4 brand-new novels every month and be billed just $4.49 per book in the U.S. or $4.99 per book in Canada. That's a saving of at least 22% off the cover price. It's quite a bargain! Shipping and handling is just 50¢ per book in the U.S. and 75¢ per book in Canada.* I understand that accepting the 2 free books and gifts places me under no obligation to buy anything. I can always return a shipment and cancel at any time. Even if I never buy another book, the two free books and gifts are mine to keep forever.

102/302 IDN FEHF

Name	(PLEASE PRINT)	
Address		Apt. #
City	State/Prov.	Zip/Postal Code

Signature (if under 18, a parent or guardian must sign)

Mail to the Reader Service:
IN U.S.A.: P.O. Box 1867, Buffalo, NY 14240-1867
IN CANADA: P.O. Box 609, Fort Erie, Ontario L2A 5X3
Not valid for current subscribers to Love Inspired Historical books.

Want to try two free books from another series?
Call 1-800-873-8635 or visit www.ReaderService.com.

* Terms and prices subject to change without notice. Prices do not include applicable taxes. Sales tax applicable in N.Y. Canadian residents will be charged applicable taxes. Offer not valid in Quebec. This offer is limited to one order per household. All orders subject to credit approval. Credit or debit balances in a customer's account(s) may be offset by any other outstanding balance owed by or to the customer. Please allow 4 to 6 weeks for delivery. Offer available while quantities last.

Your Privacy—The Reader Service is committed to protecting your privacy. Our Privacy Policy is available online at www.ReaderService.com or upon request from the Reader Service.

We make a portion of our mailing list available to reputable third parties that offer products we believe may interest you. If you prefer that we not exchange your name with third parties, or if you wish to clarify or modify your communication preferences, please visit us at www.ReaderService.com/consumerschoice or write to us at Reader Service Preference Service, P.O. Box 9062, Buffalo, NY 14269. Include your complete name and address.

LIH11B